PAUL GOBLE

THE GIRL WHO LOVED WILD HORSES

THE GIRL WHO LOVED WILD HORSES

Story and Illustrations by PAUL GOBLE

Aladdin Paperbacks

Aladdin Paperbacks
An imprint of Simon & Schuster
Children's Publishing Division
1230 Avenue of the Americas, New York, NY 10020. Copyright © 1978 by Paul Goble. All rights reserved including the right of reproduction in whole or in part in any form. Second Aladdin Paperbacks edition, 1993. Also available in a hardcover edition from Simon & Schuster Books for Young Readers. The text of this book is set in 12 pt. Century Schoolbook. The illustrations are in full-color pen-and-ink and water-color paintings, the black line separated by the artist from the base plates, reproduced in combined line and halftone.
Printed in Hong Kong.
20
Library of Congress Cataloging-in-Publication Data Goble, Paul. The girl who loved wild horses / story and illustrations by Paul Goble. — 2nd Aladdin Books ed. p.   cm. Summary: Though she is fond of her people, a girl prefers to live among the wild horses where she is truly happy and free. ISBN 0-689-71696-6 [1. Fairy tales.   2. Indians of North America—Fiction.   3. Horses—Fiction.] I. Title.   PZ8.G537Gi   1993   [E]—dc20   92-29560

For Janet

The people were always moving from place to place following the herds of buffalo. They had many horses to carry the tipis and all their belongings. They trained their fastest horses to hunt the buffalo.

There was a girl in the village who loved horses. She would often get up at daybreak when the birds were singing about the rising sun. She led the horses to drink at the river. She spoke softly and they followed.

People noticed that she understood horses in a special way. She knew which grass they liked best and where to find them shelter from the winter blizzards. If a horse was hurt she looked after it.

Every day when she had helped her mother carry water and collect firewood, she would run off to be with the horses. She stayed with them in the meadows, but was careful never to go beyond sight of home.

One hot day when the sun was overhead she felt sleepy. She spread her blanket and lay down. It was nice to hear the horses eating and moving slowly among the flowers. Soon she fell asleep.

A faint rumble of distant thunder did not waken her. Angry clouds began to roll out across the sky with lightning flashing in the darkness beneath. But the fresh breeze and scent of rain made her sleep soundly.

Suddenly there was a flash of lightning, a crash and rumbling which shook the earth. The girl leapt to her feet in fright. Everything was awake. Horses were rearing up on their hind legs and snorting in terror. She grabbed a horse's mane and jumped on his back.

In an instant the herd was galloping away like the wind. She called to the horses to stop, but her voice was lost in the thunder. Nothing could stop them. She hugged her horse's neck with her fingers twisted into his mane. She clung on, afraid of falling under the drumming hooves.

The horses galloped faster and faster, pursued by the thunder and lightning. They swept like a brown flood across hills and through valleys. Fear drove them on and on, leaving their familiar grazing grounds far behind.

At last the storm disappeared over the horizon. The tired horses slowed and then stopped and rested. Stars came out and the moon shone over hills the girl had never seen before. She knew they were lost.

Next morning she was wakened by a loud neighing. A beautiful spotted stallion was prancing to and fro in front of her, stamping his hooves and shaking his mane. He was strong and proud and more handsome than any horse she had ever dreamed of. He told her that he was the leader of all the wild horses who roamed the hills. He welcomed her to live with them. She was glad, and all her horses lifted their heads and neighed joyfully, happy to be free with the wild horses.

The people searched everywhere for the girl and the vanished horses. They were nowhere to be found.

But a year later two hunters rode into the hills where the wild horses lived. When they climbed a hill and looked over the top they saw the wild horses led by the beautiful spotted stallion. Beside him rode the girl leading a colt. They called out to her. She waved back, but the stallion quickly drove her away with all his horses.

The hunters galloped home and told what they had seen. The men mounted their fastest horses and set out at once.

It was a long chase. The stallion defended the girl and the colt. He circled round and round them so that the riders could not get near. They tried to catch him with ropes but he dodged them. He had no fear. His eyes shone like cold stars. He snorted and his hooves struck as fast as lightning.

The riders admired his courage. They might never have caught the girl except her horse stumbled and she fell.

She was glad to see her parents and they thought she would be happy to be home again. But they soon saw she was sad and missed the colt and the wild horses.

Each evening as the sun went down people would hear the stallion neighing sadly from the hilltop above the village, calling for her to come back.

The days passed. Her parents knew the girl was lonely. She became ill and the doctors could do nothing to help her. They asked what would make her well again. "I love to run with the wild horses," she answered. "They are my relatives. If you let me go back to them I shall be happy for evermore."

Her parents loved her and agreed that she should go back to live with the wild horses. They gave her a beautiful dress and the best horse in the village to ride.

The spotted stallion led his wild horses down from the hills. The people gave them fine things to wear: colorful blankets and decorated saddles. They painted designs on their bodies and tied eagle feathers and ribbons in their manes and tails.

In return, the girl gave the colt to her parents. Everyone was joyful.

Once again the girl rode beside the spotted stallion. They were proud and happy together.

But she did not forget her people. Each year she would come back, and she always brought her parents a colt.

And then one year she did not return and was never seen again. But when hunters next saw the wild horses there galloped beside the mighty stallion a beautiful mare with a mane and tail floating like wispy clouds about her. They said the girl had surely become one of the wild horses at last.

Today we are still glad to remember that we have relatives among the Horse People. And it gives us joy to see the wild horses running free. Our thoughts fly with them.

A Navaho's song about his horse:

My horse has a hoof like striped agate;
His fetlock is like a fine eagle-plume;
His legs are like quick lightning.
My horse's body is like an eagle-plumed arrow;
My horse has a tail like a trailing black cloud.
His mane is made of short rainbows.
My horse's ears are made of round corn.
My horse's eyes are made of big stars.
My horse's teeth are made of white shell.
The long rainbow is in his mouth for a bridle,
And with it I guide him.

Black Elk, an Oglala Sioux, had a dream in which he heard a stallion sing a song:

My horses, prancing they are coming.
My horses, neighing they are coming.
Prancing, they are coming.
All over the universe they come.
They will dance; may you behold them.
A horse nation, they will dance,
May you behold them.

5-Image Prism

3-Image Prism, Orange Filter, 4-Point Star

5-Image Prism, Rotated During Exposure

No Filter

Yellow Filter

No Filter

Orange Filter

Infrared Film, Magenta Filter

Infrared Film, Yellow Filter

Yellow/Mauve Color Back Filter (Cokin/Minolta)

Star Filter (Cokin/Minolta) ⟶

Multiple Image (Cokin/Minolta)

No Filter (Tiffen)

Color Graduated, Brown Filter (Tiffen)

5-Image Prism, 6-Point Star

104

Vari-Color (Tiffen) **Vari-Color (Tiffen)**

Center Spot (Tiffen)

Polarizing Filter (Cokin/Minolta)

Double Mask (Cokin/Minolta)

Center Spot (Cokin/Minolta)

Orange Filter

Pre-Shaped Frame (Cokin/Minolta)

No Filter, Type B Film (Tiffen)

Fluorescent Light Filter, Type B Film (Tiffen)

3-Image Filter

No Filter (Cokin/Minolta)

Fog Filter (Cokin/Minolta)

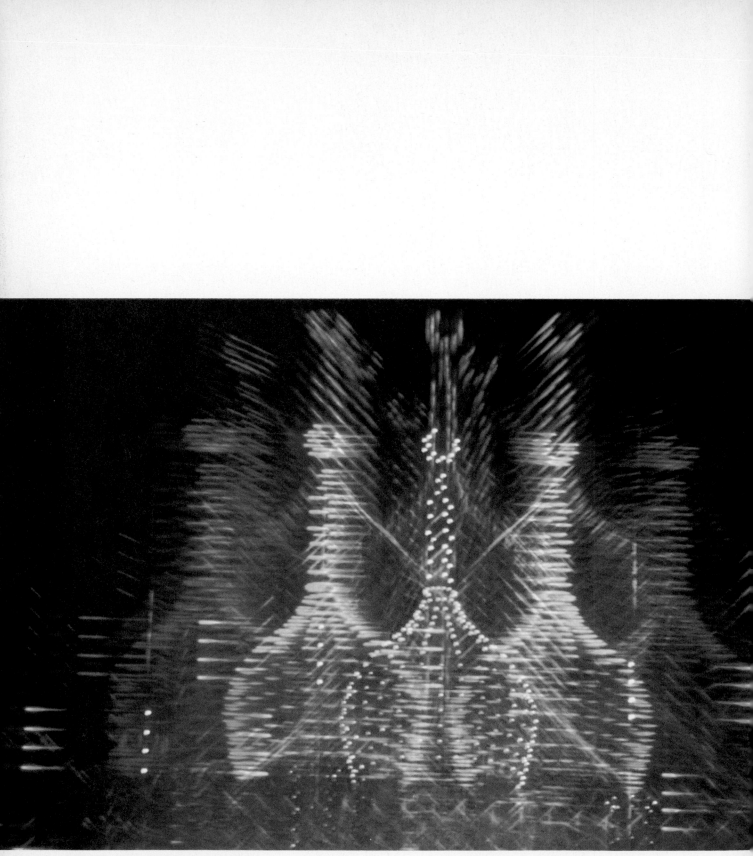

Diffraction Filter—Vari-Burst I (Tiffen)

3P Multiple-Image (Tiffen)

Diffraction Filter—Vari-Burst I (Tiffen)

4-Point Star (Tiffen)

Diffraction Filter—Vari-Burst II (Tiffen)

No Filter (Tiffen)

Fog Filter 3 (Tiffen)

112

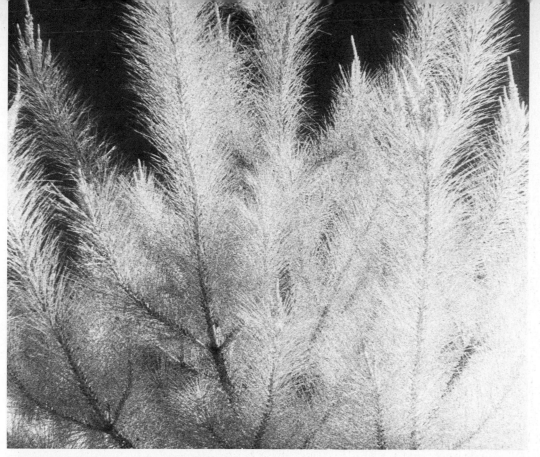

Infrared Film, Red Filter (Mike Stensvold)

Infrared Film, Red Filter (Mike Stensvold)

Split–Color Filters

Three types of split-color filters are offered by Hoya, Prinz and other filter manufacturers: 1) half color; 2) dual or bicolor; 3) tricolor. All contain one or more pieces of gelatin filter material which has been sandwiched between two optical glass plates to form a filter laminate. They are not graduated filters, but contain a sharp break between color and clear or colored areas. Manipulation of this sharp color border, as we'll see shortly, is done by the choice of lens used (focal length) and aperture. For maximum versatility, the laminate is mounted in a rotating frame, just as a polarizing filter. This allows the colors to be positioned in front of the lens according to the requirements of your subject.

Half Color

These 50 percent clear and 50 percent colored filters are offered in a variety of shades covering all primary and complementary colors, as well as two shades of gray. Half color filters are designed primarily for use with color film, although some of the colors can be used as split-field contrast filters with black-and-white emulsions, provided that the subject will accommodate the effect.

Dual or Bicolor

These two-tone filters are similar to the half color variety, but contain two contrasting colors which are usually deeper in hue. They are used

to provide color contrast in foreground/background, land/sea, land/sky and similar subjects.

Tricolor

Add one more color section to the dual filters and you have a three-section or tricolor filter. These are available in two different types: triangle and parallel. The triangle type usually contains triangular wedges of the three primary colors—red, blue and green. The parallel filter looks like a color version of the 3P prism attachment, since it contains strips of blue, yellow and pink, as shown in Figure 1.

Varying the Effect

There are two ways to control the effect of split-color filters: focal length and aperture. When used with shorter focal length (wide-angle) lenses, the border between the color segments will appear fairly sharp and definite. But as you move into telephoto focal lengths, this distinct border gradually becomes a blend of the colors involved. When half color filters are used with telephoto lenses, the clear section dilutes the hue of the colored section at the border, resulting in a graduated color effect.

The color border will blend at wide apertures when split-color filters are used with a normal lens, becoming more distinct as you stop the lens down. The amount of blending at large apertures is less with wide-angle lenses, and somewhat greater with telephoto lenses. To get a good working grasp of the effect and how it's controlled, you should experiment with several different focal lengths and aperture settings.

Calculating Exposure

You can use half color filters with no increase

Above left:
Taken with an 85mm lens, no filter. Deep-blue sky is washed out in this straight print, with only a hint of clouds. Green foreground is sufficiently dark. To improve this picture, sky would have to be burned in during printing.

Left:
Taken with an orange/green bicolor filter at f/8. Orange half brings out clouds and sky, while green half lightens foreground foliage for better contrast in this straight print. No darkroom controls are required to obtain this result.

in exposure. The dual and tricolor filters are assigned exposure factors according to the color combination. These are called standard factors, as they represent an average of the two or three different colors involved. Obviously, an exposure factor for these filters can be nothing more than a starting point. Your subject, its highlight/shadow ratio, background and the arrangement of the filter colors all play a part in determining a proper exposure. For this reason, I'd suggest that you bracket a series of three shots in one-stop increments when you are using dual or tricolor filters.

Appropriate Subjects

You'll find dual color filters most useful with subjects that contain a strong center line, whether vertical or horizontal. City skyline, beach scenic or architectural/landscape shots with large expanses of foreground/background are some of the less complex ones that come to mind.

Tricolor filters require a bit more imagination to use effectively. The parallel variety work best when there are semi-distinct divisions between foreground, mid-area and background. Finding two vertical division lines appropriately spaced can be difficult. The triangle type tends to produce more of a multicolored wash than the pie-shaped segments suggested by its appearance.

Experimention is also the name of the game with dual and tricolor filters. Try combining two dual color filters and you'll be able to work with four different colors in one filter. You can control the size of the segments by positioning of the two filters relative to each other. Tricolor filters can also be used in pairs with interesting effects.

Half color filters will add color to an overcast sky, produce a pseudo-sunset effect in landscape and beach scenes, add color to an expanse of water in the foreground, etc.

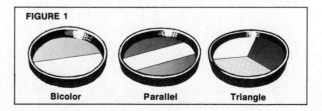

FIGURE 1

Bicolor   Parallel   Triangle

Diffraction Filters

This family of special-effect filters constitutes one of the most popular lens attachments for amateur photographers. A large variety of diffraction filters is currently available under various trade and brand names, but all are descendants of the original transmission diffraction grating concept introduced about a decade ago. To see how they work, let's take a look at the diffraction grating concept and its offspring, the holographic laser filter—tools that can help transform an ordinary photograph into one that's extraordinary, provided they are used properly.

There are two basic types of diffraction gratings available—transmission and reflective. The transmission grating allows light to pass through it and can thus be used over a camera lens as a filter. But reflective grating material is basically opaque and is used primarily as background material to reflect spectra in a most unusual way to enhance fashion or product shots.

A diffraction grating is a piece of glass or plastic material which contains thousands (12,000 or more per inch) of precise lines etched on its surface—much like the new video disc, but the lines on diffraction gratings are parallel, not circular. Since the lines create ridges and grooves on the grating surface, they function like thousands of tiny prisms. Light rays from a point light source which pass through the grating are diffracted or bent, causing flare across the lines. This is due to interference among the wavelengths of light, causing each to leave the grating's surface at a different angle. By decomposing the light spectrum in this manner, the colors of the spectrum are created from "white" light without deforming the image.

Since the grating lines are parallel, so are the flare lines, which appear in opposite directions from the highlights. The violet rays appear nearest to the light source, followed by the blue, green, yellow and red. How much color will be produced depends upon the spacing of the grating lines and the angle at which the camera lens sees them. Since the majority of light which forms the image on the film passes through the grating unchanged, most grating materials produce a relatively subtle effect.

Diffraction gratings were originally made by engraving thousands of lines on optically flat glass plates. But this technique is costly, so the engraved glass plate is used as a "master" to make plastic reproductions in much the same manner that record companies "press" thousands of discs from a single master. Manufactured from acetate, transmission diffraction grating material is available in inexpensive sheets or rolls and can be cut to size to fit a gelatin filter frame. Using the material in a filter gel frame assures that the grating will be held in front of the lens in a single flat plane, and also helps to protect it from fingerprints, scratches and other contamination which may affect its surface.

Holographic diffraction gratings are more complex than the ordinary grating. Often called laser filters, these contain "families" of parallel lines produced by the interference pattern of laser light. These families cross each other, resulting in the creation of several orders of spectra and images. The effect is far more elaborate, abstract and spectacular than that of the ordinary diffraction grating.

Since they produce a multi-image effect, you can use a laser filter with virtually any subject, but the most eye-catching effect results when a specular reflection or point light source is included in the picture. Laser filters can presently be categorized in five major groups, each of which produces a distinctly different effect.

1. *Linear* produces a unidirection and repetitive pattern. This pattern is produced on both sides of a point light source along a straight line. The result is a visible ghostly image on each side of the main image.

2. *Radial* emanates a light spindle pattern from the point light source, much like the spokes of a wheel. The grid generally creates three orders of diffracted light, the pattern of whch can be changed by rotation of the filter, variation of the camera angle, lighting or subject movement. Constant filter rotation during exposure will create the effect of motion, which can enhance a static subject.

3. *Circular* surrounds the light source with ever-increasing rings of solid color. If the light source is centered in a rectangular negative for-

Right:
Diffraction effects differ according to filter type and usage. They are used to best advantage with color slide film, which emphasizes the prism effect.

Prinz Rainbow

Tiffen Vari-Burst

Spectralstar 18X

Spectralstar 8X

Spectralstar 8X & 18X combined

Spectralstar 8X, 18X and Tiffen Vari-Burst

117

mat, the outer rings will be cut off by the frame edge. A square negative format is necessary to capture the entire effect.

4. *Nebula* radiates a multistreak burst pattern from the point light source to form a circle. This color "spray" produces a fuller pattern than the radial, and will also form a near solid pattern by constant slow rotation during a long exposure.

5. *Rainbow* spreads the point light source rays into a starburst design with two to three orders of spectra. Some varieties contain a clear center spot surrounded by the prismatic plastic. These are generally more delicate in effect.

Actually, the descriptions above are only very rough approximations of the various effects possible, and as the state of the art advances, more and different types are certain to appear. Some diffraction filters work most effectively

with the lens wide open, while others require that you stop down considerably for the full effect. In this respect, they're much like cross screens, star filters and prism attachments.

Experimentation is paramount, and that's one of the major reasons they're so very popular these days—the effects have not yet been completely exhausted and you can still "do your own thing" without feeling that everyone else has done it before you. As with the previously mentioned filters and attachments, you'll probably end up with several different diffraction filters before you're satiated with the possible effects.

Those who wish to fit a large-diameter lens mount at a reasonable cost, or who use filter gels as a matter of course, will find the diffraction grating sheets most practical. These are available from several sources, including Edmund Scientific Company, 100 Edscorp Building, Barrington, New Jersey 08007. This company is constantly coming up with new and different designs in prismatic arrangement.

By using the sheet material, you can outfit either a circular or full-frame fisheye lens to produce some really mind-blowing effects. Simply place the camera on a tripod so that you can use both hands. Set and release the self-timer, then use the 8-10-second interval to position the sheet of grating material in front of the lens in a U shape, where it should remain fixed during the exposure.

This material also works beautifully with special-effect cameras such as the Panon Widelux, as you need cut only a small piece from one end and fasten it to the moving lens cylinder with cellophane tape to hold it in place for the entire exposure over a 140-degree field of view. I've also taped small pieces over the lens of a 110 pocket camera to achieve rather interesting effects on the tiny 13x17mm format.

While most manufacturers recommend a slight exposure increase when using their diffraction, laser or rainbow filters, I'd suggest that you experiment with exposures as well as with subjects and effects. You'll find a slight degree of underexposure highly desirable for maximum color saturation when working against a light background. When you use a diffraction filter for night shots, it's a good idea to stay with the basic exposure recommended without the filter, as this will help to intensify the color saturation against the dark of night.

Left:
A Prinz Rainbow combined with a 5-segment prism highlights the fantasy called the Las Vegas Strip.

You'll find that a given filter will not be effective with every subject—another reason for eventually owning several instead of just one. Depending upon the number and kind of reflections in your subject, diffraction filters will deliver an effect ranging from a wavy line of long rainbow colors to a complete matrix of rainbow crosses intersecting every bright highlight or point light source.

Try to match the effect to the subject instead of simply using it with whatever comes in front of your camera. For really different effects, try combining a diffraction filter with a prism attachment or a star filter. If you're into one of the filter systems, you might want to investigate a prism filter. These are not available in series or screw-in types and work best with subjects containing a lot of contrast, as this permits greater separation of the color fringing. But whatever you do with diffraction filters, do it with taste and flair, and you'll be amazed at how much they can add to the fun and flavor of your hobby.

FULLY AUTOMATIC CAMERAS AND DIFFRACTION FILTERS

A growing number of sophisticated 35mm SLR cameras are fully automatic in exposure control, with no manual mode provided. While such cameras are a boon to many amateurs, they can also result in less-than-satisfactory pictures when using diffraction, cross screen or star filters. When subjects that contain areas of intense light are photographed at night, the meter may select a shutter speed/lens opening combination that leads to overexposure of the bright areas. When this happens, the filter's effect will be considerably diminished.

If the camera has a one- or two-stop compensation device, use it—underexposure is preferable to overexposure when working with such filters. Cameras not equipped with such an override pose a real problem. In this case, shoot several pictures from different points of view, changing the composition. One or more suitable slides should result from this practice.

Chromatic and Dichroic Color Filters

Following the introduction of the original Cromofilter concept a few years back, several variations of the chromatic image filter have appeared on the market under a variety of tradenames. All are expensive, require a good deal of imagination to use effectively and can be confusing to the beginner who isn't able to catch the basic operating principle behind a particular brand—what will he get if he spends the money? To answer that question and clarify the entire chromatic image filter, we'll delve into the various systems in this chapter, beginning with the original filter concept which started the stampede.

Chromofilters

It was still summer when French fashion photographer Jean Coquin was hired to photo-graph Pierre Cardin's autumn fashions a few years ago. Since the idea was to do an outdoor photo session, Coquin found it necessary to find some means of faking fall in a realistic manner. Recalling the principle of a prewar graduated filter once manufactured by Rollei, Coquin devised his own series of graduated filters in various colors and hues. These would permit both local color modification and the introduction of other desired colors wherever he required them. His idea was so innovative that it became commercially available during 1975 under the tradename Cromofilter.

Cromofilters are distributed in this country by Argraph Corp., and a variety of Japanese imitations and variations have made their appearance, with more certain to follow. Along with the diffraction filters, Cromofilters are one of the

hottest filter concepts presently on the market. The Cromofilters (and their imitators) are manufactured of optical resin 1.6mm thick. This material accepts colorations which are difficult if not impossible to incorporate in glass. The resin material has two other virtues—it's perfectly plane parallel and is almost as hard as glass.

One-half of the filter is tinted a particular color, with the remaining half graduated to neutral. Manufactured in threaded rotating mounts, the tinted half can be positioned where desired, preventing color overlap between two different picture areas by following a subject mass line such as the horizon. A second filter of a different color can also be threaded into the first, producing a two-color effect. When used in this manner, a narrow neutral strip separates the two tinted areas.

Fourteen different filters are offered in seven colors—neutral gray, blue, yellow, pink, mauve, tobacco and emerald. Each color is available in two densities—Series 1 (0.45) and Series 2 (0.75). Used in conjunction with a particular filter color, the neutral gray increases local density without affecting its color. The neutral gray can also be used to reduce the intensity of a bright subject area without affecting the color. For example, that pale blue sky might be exactly right but too bright. Using the neutral gray filter will reduce the brightness of the sky without losing its delicate blue coloration.

To help you grasp the importance of local color modification on color slides, here are a few other suggestions where Cromofilters can offer corrective help and create striking moods or effects. You can:

1. Neutralize a color by introducing its complementary color—a pink filter will neutralize an expanse of grass or other foliage.

2. Simulate moonlight in daylight by darkening the sky with a filter while underexposing the foreground.

3. Add color contrast in areas adjacent to the main subject.

4. Strengthen the color of either foreground or background—or both.

Left:
Chromatic filters offer considerable control in providing local color modification. With a subject like this, you can strengthen either sky or water color by using a graduated filter.

5. Darken the background to emphasize the subject.

6. Add dramatic effect by darkening just the sky.

7. Change the mood by inserting specific colors—a touch of yellow will warm a winter sky while mauve will increase its apparent coldness.

8. Enhance the mood by inserting specific colors—a touch of pink or tobacco will richen the color hues of a sunset or sunrise.

The list is endless, but I'm sure that you've caught on to the versatility of Coquin's concept and can see why it's become so very popular with photographers the world around, as well as so often imitated.

The use of Cromofilters and their imitators requires some care in exposure if you wish the full effect. When used on an SLR with a built-in metering system, they will cause some overexposure of the foreground unless the camera's meter reading is adjusted manually. If the 0.45 density is used, close the lens down ½ stop beyond that recommended by the camera. For the 0.75 density filters, close down a full stop.

The most efficient way to correct exposure is to take a reading before installing the filter to the lens, or by using a hand-held meter. Regardless of color or density, when two filters are used to correct both foreground and background, you should expose just as you would if no filtration were involved.

Since Cromofilters are fairly expensive, it's not a good idea to buy the entire set at one time—even if you can afford it. I'd recommend that you begin with the 0.45 density in neutral gray and blue, and build from this point. A useful accumulation of Cromofilters would include both neutral grays (0.45 and 0.75 densities), a 0.45 blue, 0.75 tobacco, 0.45 emerald, and one other—pink, mauve, or yellow in either density as preferred.

This selection will permit you to work with the majority of situations you'll encounter and give you a good feeling for the effects in which you've invested your money. As with most of the other special-effect filters, the careful use of a Cromofilter will strengthen the mood or intensity of a scene, but used indiscriminately, the results will be meaningless and visually distracting, if not downright annoying.

Dichroic Polarizers

This type of chromatic image filter is best represented by the Izumar Chromostar, distributed in this country by Spiratone under its Colorflow trademark. The Chromostar/Colorflow concept is available in two different versions—a single color and a bicolor mode. In the single-color version, the color produced by the filter varies from dense to an almost transparent hue as the filter is rotated in its frame. The bicolor version also changes color in this manner as the filter is rotated in its mount, but continued rotation will carry through a change to a second color. For example, rotating the red-blue filter changes the color from dark to light red, through magenta and then light to dark blue—all done with just one filter.

How do they work? On the principle of dichroic polarization. The single-color version consists of a double glass filter. Its rear element is a normal polarizer, while the front one has a polarizer bonded to it. Rotating the front element causes the intensity of its color to change from light to dark.

The bicolor version is considerably more complex, as its front element contains a polarizer, the color filter and a plastic dichroic layer. Light passing through the first polarizer and color filter is twisted into red, blue or green light rays at varying angles by the dichroic layer, as shown in Figure 1. With the red/blue filter, for example, the dichroic layer is magenta, leaving only red and blue rays at different angles (magenta absorbs the green rays). Which one of the two colors will pass through the second polarizer depends upon its position. Thus, rotating the front element causes its hue or color to change from red to blue to red again, with all the variations between the two.

Since the single-color version amounts to a variable-density filter, any of the six colors available can also be used in black-and-white photography. The single-color filter is to a normal black-and-white contrast filter as a zoom lens is to a fixed focal length. Two or three individual lenses will provide the most often used focal lengths, but the zoom lens gives every in-between focal length at the twist of a ring. Two or three single-color contrast filters will provide the most often used filtration, but the variable-density filter offers every in-between degree of filtration—filtration available in no other way. With color film, the single version will warm up shots made in bluish daylight, cope with fluorescent lights, deepen pale sunsets/sunrises—you name it.

The bicolor filter offers vibrant, intensive and even unreal effects. For example, the main part of your subject will be one color while other parts show a different hue. Let's suppose that you're photographing a building against a blue sky. Rotate the filter to give the sky a general blue hue. The building, which does not reflect polarized light, will appear normal, but its windows will contain a red hue. Rotate the filter again and the sky becomes red while the windows change to blue. In case you haven't caught on yet to the trick, it's the differing angles of polarization that account for the switch in colors.

Reflections on different planes within the subject will also take on different colors. Photo-

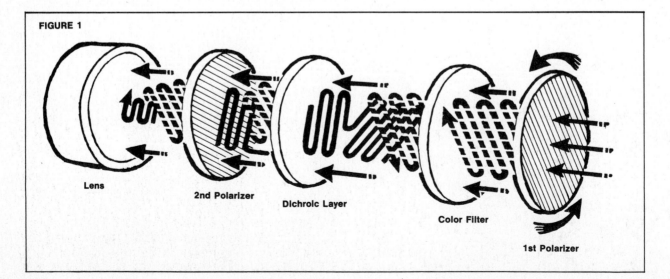

FIGURE 1

Lens

2nd Polarizer

Dichroic Layer

Color Filter

1st Polarizer

graph a car with a highly waxed finish on a wet road or pavement. The car windows will show one hue, the side of the vehicle a different one and the road still another.

Rotating the entire bicolor filter itself instead of just the front element will also change the effect. Set the filter at its median or neutral position and back the entire filter off the lens mount up to one full turn—how much depends upon the effect you already have and what you want. In this way, you can even obtain a tricolored effect. Both the single and bicolor filters can be used with infrared color film to obtain effects not possible with conventional filters.

Below:
Bicolor dichroic polarizers will produce a wide variety of effects. The difference between blue (photo No. 1) and red (photo No. 2) is shown here.

Due to the nature of their construction, the dichroic polarizers are fairly thick and should not be used on lenses of 35mm or shorter focal lengths (35mm cameras) because of a tendency to vignette. You'll have no problems with 40mm or longer focal lengths, but don't try to double these up with another type of attachment such as a prism or you may well run head-on into the vignetting problem.

Exposure is another area of consideration. The single-color version is not too dense and thus will not require the heavy exposure compensation of the bicolor version. Using a bicolor filter in bright sunlight with ASA 64 color film will result in exposures in the range of 1/15-1/60 second at f/4, according to the subject and the amount of color you dial in by rotating the filter. If depth of field or subject-stopping shutter

1

2

speeds are considerations, you might want to use one of the faster color films available, such as Kodak Ektachrome ED 200 or EL 400.

Those 35mm cameras which use a beam splitter in their metering system (Canon SLR, Prakticas, Leicaflexes) will be utterly faked out by the selective polarization of both types of dichroic color filter. What compensation the camera's meter does make for the placement of a bicolor filter in the light path is just a starting point. Bracketing your exposures has the advantage of providing a slight under- and overexposure, which might well turn up a picture that is more pleasing than one that was properly exposed. Such experimentation is necessary in any case, if you wish to determine exactly what a dichroic color filter will do and take full advantage of its versatility.

You might have some problem focusing slower lenses when a bicolor filter is used. If so, don't focus without the filter and then install it to take the picture, as there's bound to be some amount of focus shift from the thickness of the filter. You'll find the split-image rangefinder screen easiest to use, especially in dim light or at apertures slower than f/4—another reason for using one of the faster color films.

To this point, I've discussed the dichroic color filters mainly in terms of the Izumar/Spiratone Colorflow concept. The Spiratone versions are sold in mounts which are calibrated from 0 to 10, allowing you to return exactly to a particular setting—especially handy if you're fooling around to see if you can find an effect more or less pronounced than the one you may have decided on.

Like the Izumar Chromostar, the original Spiratone Colorflow filters were a single unit which contained all of the polarizers needed to obtain the effect. Current Colorflow filters are designated as Colorflow II and have adopted a "modular" approach, which means that they come without the rear polarizer—you must furnish it in order to have the filter function properly. This has lowered the cost per filter, since you're not paying for a polarizer with every Colorflow II you buy.

Other dichroic color filters are offered by Prinz, Hoya and Vivitar. The Vivitar Chromo Blend filters are also modular, thus they must be used with a separate polarizing filter in order to achieve the color-changing effect. If you use a Chromo Blend or Colorflow filter, remember to install the polarizer on the camera lens first, then fit the filter to the polarizer. The Prinz Verio Color and Hoya Vari PL-Color are both very similar to the original Colorflow Type II/Izumar Bicolor but lack the calibration scale of the Colorflow filter.

Which filter type is better—the integral or modular? This depends in part upon your pocketbook and your working habits. The modular will save you money, since the same polarizing filter will be used with all color dichroic filters you buy. They also require less storage space and, if used with one of the thin polarizers, are not as apt to cause vignetting with shorter focal length lenses.

Yet the integral type does have a benefit or two for those of us who seem unable to find something as simple as a polarizing filter in our gadget bag at the exact moment we need it. True,

1

2

Dichroic polarizers can play some tricks on you, as shown here. When the filter is rotated to a full blue position (photo No. 1), the mountains and cloud layer in the background disappear completely. Switching to a full red position (photo No. 2) alters tonal re- *lationships but brings both mountains and clouds into view. You won't notice this effect in the viewfinder, so remember what each color will do to objects reflecting the same color.*

the rear polarizer included within each filter has no other value, but it does preclude the possibility that you'll throw the dichroic filter in your gadget bag or pocket only to forget the polarizer necessary to make it work.

The uses to which I've alluded thus far should keep you busy experimenting for months just to discover what one or more dichroic color filters will do, but these are by no means the end of the list. These filters can be used in slide copying to alter your original, adding color or correcting filtration errors. They are also very useful in black-and-white copy work where there may be a slight residue of a stained original left on the copy negative because the absorption pattern of your contrast filter did not equal the transmission pattern of the stain. With a dichroic color filter instead of a single-color contrast filter, you can match the filter's shade exactly to any stains on the original and be able to eliminate them completely with one release of your shutter button.

Dichroic color filters are most easily used with SLR cameras, since you can see and study the exact effect of filter position through the viewfinder, changing it slightly if necessary to increase or decrease the coloration. But this doesn't mean the rangefinder camera owner must forego the exciting possibilities such filters offer just because of his optical viewfinder. Like standard polarizing filters, the dichroic type can be used by rotating them in front of your eye until you see the effect desired. At this point, simply transfer the filter from your eye to the camera's lens mount without changing its relative position. This method is not 100-percent foolproof, as there's bound to be some slight degree of movement in the process of mounting the filter on the lens, but the slight change in alignment should not prove a major disrupting factor.

You'll find the yellow/blue and red/blue bicolor and the single-color red filters to be most practical at the outset. The yellow/blue will take the place of an entire set of 81/82 light balancing filters for correcting outdoor pictures, while the red/blue will add appropriate color to most subjects. The single-color red performs a variety of tasks, including the replacement of a CC10R for removing blue, green or cyan from outdoor shadows, substituting perfectly for a skylight (1A) filter, and taking the place of a red contrast filter in black-and-white photography. Beyond this basic selection, you're on your own to open the doors to color creativity whenever and wherever you want or need it.

EYEBALLING FILTER SELECTION

Successful filter usage with black-and-white film depends to a great extent upon the photographer's ability to visualize a scene *without* its color content. Like dating beautiful women, some have an instinctive flair for it while others never do catch on to how it's done. It's not a simple feat, nor is it something you can learn overnight, but if you can at least partially master it by virtue of time and experience, the end results are well worth the effort in terms of improved photographs.

Ever watch an artist at work? The skilled ones often survey that before them through half-closed eyes. It's a way of subliminating much of the minute detail, enabling them to concentrate on shapes and masses which compose the subject. It's also a way of reducing color brightness. Although pastels are less affected than the deeper hues, a great deal depends upon the ambient light, color groupings and the arrangement. Once you learn the trick, you also have to know how to interpret what you see.

Viewing filters are often used to help suppress color and allow the photographer to make objective value judgments. Looking at the scene through a neutral density filter will lower the overall scene brightness. A dark yellow or monochromatic viewing filter will kill all color differences in a scene, and these are often used by Hollywood technicians to help them arrange lighting on a studio set.

Panchromatic vision filters alter the eye's sensitivity to approximately the same as that of a pan film emulsion. By looking through this purple filter *and* the filter you wish to use, you'll see the scene almost exactly as the film does. Last but not least, a Kodak No. 90 (olive-colored) filter is also useful in helping to reduce color brightness and let you study the tonal values. Regardless of which approach you favor, you'll have to work with it, keep notes on your observations and compare the notes with the results if you expect to become proficient at the art of selecting the proper filter by visualization.

Split-Field and Dual-Image Filters

The filters discussed in this chapter are special ones which will produce certain effects not easily obtained in any other manner. Although either filter type can be fitted to virtually any camera, both are most easily used with a reflex type, whether of single- or twin-lens design. The SLR is preferable, of course, since it permits direct viewing through the lens, which simplifies the problems of composition and focus. When used with a TLR, the filter must be placed over the viewing lens while arranging, focusing and composing your picture. It is then transferred to the taking lens before the shutter is released to take the picture.

Using either of these filters with a rangefinder or other type camera with a direct optical viewfinder requires a bit of guessing and some good luck to obtain results that are "right on the button." To use the split-field lens, you must refer to the table on page 131 to find the proper subject-to-close-up-lens distance. With the dual-image filter, some leeway should be provided in subject placement to compensate for the lack of precision in the viewfinder, but with care and planning, good results can generally be obtained.

Split-Field Lenses

These are nothing more than half of a close-up lens mounted in a standard circular filter

Below:
Double exposures are easy with system filters. The dividing line can be positioned precisely where desired. (Courtesy Minolta Corporation)

ring. Offered in +½, +1, +2, +3 and +4 di-opter strengths, split-field lenses are identical with close-up lenses of the same power, as discussed in Chapter 19. Since half of the filter ring contains no glass, it provides a practical and easy way to obtain two different fields of focus in the same picture—one very close and one at normal distance.

Small subjects close to the camera can be combined with normal-size subjects located in the mid-foreground or background area—with both in sharp focus. Used properly, the split-field lens will also create extreme depth of field without revealing how it was obtained. There are many other creative uses for this particular filter, but to find them requires a certain amount of imagination. It's far too easy to stick with the usual ''sharp-flower-in-the-foreground, sharp-building-in-the-background'' type of picture with which most manufacturers advertise their split-field lenses.

Take advantage of perspective and relative image sizes to produce some startling photographs. For example, you might position a model in the background in such a way as to have her appear to be posing for a camera which is

Dual-image filters are also available in standard threaded mounts. This is the Kalt version.

many times larger than she is. Or you might use the +½ diopter split-field lens with an 85-105mm telephoto. This will produce a head-and-shoulders shot in which everything, including the background, is sharp.

One caution when using split-field lenses—watch placement of the dividing line between the diopter segment and the clear area. If it is incorrectly placed, you'll end up with an out-of-focus line that's annoyingly visible. Try to place your subjects so that the division line will blend in with a light or dark mass which contains as little detail as possible. The division line doesn't necessarily have to rest along the horizontal; if your subject matter will permit it, you can arrange the line at any angle between horizontal and vertical. Just make sure that it follows some natural break in the composition.

To complicate matters even further (and stretch your creativity), you should attempt to keep the subjects well inside their appropriate halves of the filter. If they are too close to the division line, or if there are strong point light sources on either side near the line, it's possible that they might refract along the division. This could result in semi-doughnut configurations or even double straight lines. Subject and division line placement are the primary difficulties encountered when working with a nonreflex camera. In such cases, you'll either have to carefully set up the shot and then hope for the best, or try several different combinations in hopes that one of them will work out satisfactorily.

When working with a reflex camera, adjust your focus on the subject within the clear half of the filter first. Once everything is set in that area, focus the close-up subject either by manipulating the subject itself, or by moving the camera back and forth to obtain the desired sharpness. Of course, the use of a tripod is highly recommended for precision in framing and focusing.

Once you have the close-up subject in sharp focus, recheck the clear half to make sure that everything is still satisfactory; if not, readjust until it is. Try to work at the smallest practical lens opening. If your lens can be closed down to f/22 or f/32, use these stops when lighting conditions and film speed permit a suitable corresponding shutter speed. If your lens only closes to f/16, try to work at that stop, but don't open up to more than f/11 under any circumstances or you'll run into some depth-of-field problems.

Dual-Image Filter

This unusual filter contains a totally opaque half-section which blocks off 50 percent of the picture area during exposure. By rotating the filter 180 degrees to reposition the opaque area and then making a second exposure, two half-frame pictures will blend into a single picture. Some of the effects made possible by use of the dual-image filter are shown on these pages, but they by no means exhaust the variety of trick pictures which you can produce.

To make your blends as perfect as possible (and thus hide how you made the picture), use

a tripod and set the lens to the f-stop specified below:

35mm Cameras	6x6cm Cameras
35mm lens at f/5.6	45mm lens at f/8
50-58mm lens at f/11	75-85mm lens at f/16
100-105mm lens at f/22	200mm lens at f/32

Aperture settings other than those listed may result in less-than-perfect blends—either an overlap of the two sections or a gap between the two halves. If one of these defects should turn up in your pictures even though you used the specified opening, shoot a trial series of exposures at half-stop intervals to cover a ±2-stop bracket around the supposedly correct stop. Thus, if you're using a 50mm lens on a

The dual-image filter can be used to express different facets of the same personality, as well as for pure trick photography. In photo No. 1 the dividing line is the lamp post, while in photo No. 2 it is the center of the subject's profile.

A split-field lens can be oriented as desired to permit both close and distant focus in the same picture area. Focusing on the sign in photo No. 1 results in an out-of-focus watch at the left, but add a +2 diopter split-field lens positioned vertically and the watch comes into sharp focus as well.

35mm camera, the "correct" f-stop is f/8. Bracket a series as follows: f/4, f/4-5.6, f/5.6, f/5.6-8, f/8, f/8-11, f/11, f/11-16, f/16. A quick look at the proof sheet will tell you exactly which lens opening to use in future dual-image shots.

Before using the dual-image filter, it's a good idea to block out in your mind exactly how the effect will look and how you're going to place the subject. Mount the camera on a sturdy tripod and fit the filter to the lens. Set the aperture to the required opening and rotate the opaque section of the filter into place while looking through the viewfinder. You can block off any half of the picture area—right, left, upper, lower, or diagonal—as long as your subject permits a second exposure with the opposing half blocked off.

Reopen the lens and determine the correct shutter speed for the f-stop/film speed in use. Set the camera's shutter speed dial to that speed—auto exposure cameras should be used in the manual mode. Make your first exposure, then rotate the dual image filter 180 degrees to reposition the opaque half. Recock the shutter as described below, reposition your subject and take a second exposure.

If lighting conditions are very bright or you're using a fast film on a sunny day, it may not be possible to shoot at the specified aperture, even with the highest shutter speed on your camera. In such cases, use the 2X neutral density filter included with the dual-image filter. Other filters can also be used in conjunction with the dual-image filter. Just be sure to install the dual-image filter on the lens first, then screw the other filter into it.

Most of the late-model 35mm SLR cameras have a special provision for making multiple exposures—simply throw a lever or press a button to disengage the film transport while you cock the shutter with the film advance lever. Older cameras without this provision can be used to make multiple exposures by following this procedure: Take up the slack in the film cartridge by turning the rewind knob and holding it while you make your first exposure. Still holding the rewind knob to make sure it doesn't move, depress and hold in the rewind button while cocking the shutter with the film advance lever. Make your next exposure and repeat for as many further exposures as you wish to make, releasing the rewind knob and button only prior to your final exposure.

Replace the lens cap, advance the film and release the shutter. This is known as shooting a "safety" frame and is necessary because when you throw the film advance lever after making your final exposure, the film *will not* advance a full frame. It takes a portion of the advance lever's throw to reengage the film transport, and so the film will actually move only about one-half frame or less. This "safety" frame will prevent spoiling a portion of your multiple exposure.

The purists among us may well sneer at the dual-image filter and the trick photos it provides, but there's a good deal of ingenuity possible in using it, as well as creativity. As youngsters, we used to do the same thing by hinging a piece of black cardboard to a lens hood, but working with the dual-image filter is not only easier—it's a good deal more fun!

Split-field lenses are merely one-half of a diopter lens which can be rotated according to the placement of the subject.

Close-up Lenses

Most standard or "normal" camera lenses will focus a sharp image from infinity to a point within two or three feet from the subject. When you wish to take sharp pictures at a closer camera-to-subject distance, you must use specialized equipment. If your camera has an interchangeable lens, it can be fitted with extension tubes, a bellows or a macro lens—depending upon your requirements and your budget. But you can also use inexpensive close-up lenses. These mount on the front of the camera lens in the same way as a filter. If your camera's lens is not interchangeable, these supplementary lenses are your only means of taking extreme close-ups.

Also known as plus-diopter or portrait lenses, these simple meniscus lenses optically shorten the effective focal length of your camera lens, allowing it to be focused on objects within a few

Below:
Close-up lenses can take you into an entirely new world. A variable close-up lens is especially valuable when photographing subjects like bees, since they are not likely to stay in one place too long.

TABLE 1 CLOSE-UP DATA FOR 35MM AND 6x6CM CAMERAS

Close-up Lens (diopters)	Prime Lens Focused On:	Subject to Close-up Lens (ins.)	Field of View (inches)* 50mm Lens 24 x 36mm Negative	Field of View (inches)* 75mm Lens 2¼ x 2¼ in. Negative
	Infinity	38¾	18⅝ x 28	30 x 30
	50	37	17¾ x 26⅝	28 x 28
	25	34¾	16⅝ x 25	26⅛ x 26⅛
	"Fixed"	33¾	16 x 24	25½ x 25½
	15	32⅜	15⅜ x 23	24¼ x 24¼
+1	10	29⅝	14 x 21	22 x 22
	8	27⅞	13⅛ x 19¾	20½ x 20½
	6	25½	11⅞ x 17⅞	18⅝ x 18⅝
	5	23¾	11 x 16⅝	17⅛ x 17⅛
	4	21⅝	10 x 15	15⅜ x 15⅜
	3½	20⅜	9¼ x 14	14⅜ x 14⅜
	Infinity	19½	9⅜ x 14	14¾ x 14¾
	50	19⅛	9⅛ x 13⅝	14⅜ x 14⅜
	25	18½	8⅞ x 13¼	13⅞ x 13⅞
	"Fixed"	18	8⅝ x 12⅞	13½ x 13½
	15	17¾	8½ x 12¾	13⅛ x 13⅛
+2	10	16⅞	8 x 12	12½ x 12½
	8	16⅜	7¾ x 11½	12 x 12
	6	15½	7¼ x 10⅞	11¼ x 11¼
	5	14⅞	6⅞ x 10⅜	10¾ x 10¾
	4	14	6½ x 9⅝	10 x 10
	3½	13⅜	6⅛ x 9¼	8⅞ x 8⅞
	Infinity	13	6¼ x 9⅜	9⅞ x 9⅞
	50	12⅞	6⅛ x 9¼	9⅝ x 9⅝
	25	12½	5⅞ x 8⅞	9⅜ x 9⅜
	"Fixed"	12⅜	5⅞ x 8⅞	9¼ x 9¼
	15	12¼	5¾ x 8¾	9⅛ x 9⅛
+3	10	11⅞	5⅝ x 8⅜	8¾ x 8¾
	8	11½	5⅜ x 8⅛	8⅜ x 8⅜
	6	11⅛	5⅛ x 7⅞	8 x 8
	5	10¾	4⅞ x 7½	7¾ x 7¾
	4	10⅜	4¾ x 7⅛	7⅜ x 7⅜
	3½	10	4½ x 6⅞	7 x 7
	Infinity	9⅞	4⅝ x 7	7⅜ x 7⅜
+4	"Fixed"	9½	4½ x 6⅝	7 x 7
	3½	8	3⅝ x 5⅜	5½ x 5½
	Infinity	7⅞	3¾ x 5⅝	5⅞ x 5⅞
+5	"Fixed"	7⅝	3½ x 5⅜	5⅝ x 5⅝
	3½	6½	3 x 4⅜	4½ x 4½
	Infinity	6½	3 x 4⅝	4⅞ x 4⅞
+6	"Fixed"	6⅜	3 x 4⅜	4¾ x 4¾
	3½	5⅝	2½ x 3¾	3⅞ x 3⅞
+8	Infinity	5⅛	2¼ x 3⅜	—
	4	4⅝	2 x 3	—
+10	Infinity	4¼	1⅞ x 2¾	—
	4	4	1⅝ x 2½	—

* Area is approximate, as it depends upon distance between close-up and camera lenses.
(Data courtesy of Tiffen Manufacturing Corporation)

inches of your camera. The strength or power of supplemental close-up lenses is measured in diopters from +1 to +10. The larger the diopter number, the more powerful the lens and the nearer you can move to your subject. Some manufacturers also offer fractional diopters (+¼, +½, +¾), while others provide lens attachments which cover the entire diopter range in much the same way as does a zoom lens.

As a measurement of its strength, the diopter rating of a close-up lens indicates the distance at which it will focus when the prime lens is set at infinity. For example, a +1 diopter lens will focus at precisely one meter, or about 39 inches, regardless of the focal length of the lens to which it's attached. A +2 diopter lens will focus at ½ meter, and so on to a +10 diopter, which focuses at 1/10 meter, or about 4 inches. Table 1 provides complete information on the use and effect of +1 through +10 diopter lenses when fitted to normal focal length lenses used in 35mm and medium-format photography.

As the table indicates, the field size varies according to the point of focus at which the prime

Below:
Snap-on close-up lenses are even provided for inexpensive and non-SLR cameras, but you'll have to guess at the field of view.

lens is set. The field size diminishes as the focus of the prime lens is moved toward its nearest focusing distance. When it's important to determine the proper close-up lens to use quickly, simply decide how close you wish to focus. Divide that distance in inches into 39 and the result will tell you the proper diopter to use. For example, if you want to focus at 13 inches,

Variable close-up lenses like this Prinz Varifocus Zoom cover the complete diopter range from +1 to +10. Threaded to a series adapter ring, it can be used with any SLR or TLR camera.

you'll need a +3 diopter lens (39 ÷ 13 = 3). This avoids the tedious process of trial and error.

Since the focusing range of the prime lens provides continuous coverage, each succeeding diopter will always pick up within ⅛ inch of where the previous one left off. For this reason, the + 1, + 2 and + 3 diopter lenses are often offered in sets of three. These will cover the range from 10 to 39 inches without a gap in focusing continuity. Close-up lenses can also be combined when you do not have the exact diopter needed. If this is done, add the powers to arrive at the equivalent diopter—a + 2 and a + 3 equal a + 5, etc.

It's not advisable to combine more than two such lenses, due to excessive distortion and possible vignetting. Whenever close-up lenses are combined, the strongest one should always

Below:
If you're really into close-up photography with a simple camera, this Scientific Photo Outfit provides a frame of reference for subject positioning, as well as a corrected close-up lens for use with the frame.

be attached to the camera lens first. Close-up lenses are directional and must be placed on the camera lens facing in the correct way. This is no problem with the screw-in type, but those sold in series size will have an arrow engraved on the metal ring, and this arrow must face *away* from the camera lens.

Depth of field is very shallow in close-up photography, which makes accurate focusing a must. This is not difficult with an SLR, as you're viewing through the lens. Perhaps the easiest way to establish the correct focus with a close-up lens is to place the camera within the focusing range of the diopter selected and use the prime lens's focusing ring to establish fine focus. You may find it easier to set the lens at infinity with stronger diopter lenses, adjusting the camera position instead to establish the best focus.

Cameras equipped with fixed lenses or those with rangefinders require more care in correct positioning and focusing, as what the lens sees differs from what the viewfinder shows. With such cameras, you should carefully measure

the distance between the front of the close-up lens and the subject. The camera back must be kept parallel with the subject, which should be centered in front of the lens, not the viewfinder. Using Table 1, adjust the camera's focus to the setting which corresponds with the close-up lens-to-subject distance.

Accurate camera placement requires the use of a tripod or some other firm support that will hold the camera in place without movement. With such limited depth of field, it's very difficult to hand-hold the camera at the precise distance from your subject to obtain maximum image sharpness. Moving back and forth as little as ¼ inch as you release the shutter can result in an out-of-focus image.

Below:
This series shows the field of view and depth of field when using close-up lenses.

Along with a tripod, you should use as small a lens opening as practical—not as small as possible. Remember that many camera lenses actually start to lose image definition at apertures smaller than f/11 or f/16, so don't stop down to f/22 or f/32 (if your lens permits) in the belief that you'll get a sharper picture. The loss of definition at these stops can actually offset any gain they offer in depth of field.

A fast shutter speed is very useful in preventing camera movement. To obtain the combination of fast shutter speed and small lens opening, it may be necessary to use a fast film, but don't overdo it. If an ASA 125 film will do the job, don't use an ASA 400 emulsion just for good measure. The increased grain of the faster film may well offset the gain achieved by using the faster speed/smaller opening combination. Fortunately, close-up lenses do not require any ad-

1 55mm lens at closest focusing distance of 24 inches.

2 +1 close-up lens added to normal lens.

4 +3 close-up lens added to normal lens.

5 +1, +2 and +3 close-up lenses stacked together.

ditional exposure, whether used individually or in combination.

Don't overlook the value of using a cable release or the camera's self-timer to trip the shutter as a means of minimizing camera movement. If your SLR has a mirror lock-up feature, this can be put to handy use once you've framed and focused your subject properly. By locking up the mirror to prevent any jar from mirror bounce, and using the self-timer to release the shutter and prevent movement caused by camera vibration, you'll assure yourself of the best results when using close-up lenses.

There may be some minor loss of image sharpness (especially at the edges) when using close-up lenses. However, you should be able to make an 8x10 enlargement with virtually no loss of sharpness from a 35mm negative taken with the aid of a +3 diopter lens. Of course,

fine-tuning your choice and use of film, exposure and development will hold such loss to an even smaller level.

Close-up lenses can also be used with moderate to medium telephotos to increase image size at the closest focusing distance of the lens. The close-up lens-to-subject distance will remain the same as for a normal focal length lens, but the image will increase in size in arithmetic proportion to the focal length of the telephoto used. Suppose your subject produces an image size of ¼ inch when photographed with a 50mm lens and +3 diopter lens at a lens-to-subject distance of 13 inches. Leaving everything else constant, switch to a 100mm lens and the image size will double to ½ inch; use a 200mm and the image increases to one inch. As with normal lenses, keep the aperture to about f/11 when possible, and try to avoid the use of close-up lenses above +5 diopter.

Fractional diopter close-up lenses work well with telephoto optics, since they extend the minimum focusing distance without increasing the required exposure. With lenses which focus to 12 feet (regardless of the focal length), the closest focusing distance becomes 6⅓ feet with a +¼ diopter, 4 1/6 feet with a +½ diopter, and 3 1/6 feet with a +¾ diopter lens. Minus lenses are also available in series sizes and strengths to −4 diopters. These are used to reduce the image size proportionately when it's necessary to increase the field size, but the camera cannot be moved farther away from the subject.

If you're really into close-up work, you might consider one of the zoom or variable diopter attachments. This will provide the same series of effects which are possible with a set of individual diopter lenses, but in a more convenient

3
+2 close-up lens added to normal lens.

6
55mm macro lens at 1:2 magnification.

7
55mm macro lens at 1:2 magnification with +1, +2 and +3 close-up lenses stacked together.

package. Most zoom diopter attachments function by simply rotating a ring, and will vary the magnification ratio from about that of a + 2 to a + 10 diopter lens.

When properly used, close-up lenses are in-

Below:
This series shows the use of a macro lens at 1:2 magnification with teleconverters.

valuable in the darkroom, taking the place of a second lens for those on a tight budget. Ideally, the lens should be located *above* the enlarger lens with its convex side facing toward the light source. If possible, tape the diopter lens in place over the rear element of the enlarging lens.

Using a plus-diopter lens in conjunction with

55mm macro lens at 1:2 magnification.

With 2X converter; two f-stop loss in speed.

With 3X converter; three f-stop loss in speed.

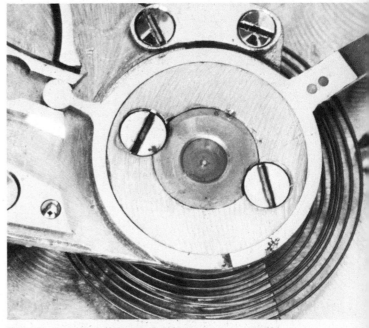

With 2X plus 3X converters; five f-stop loss in speed.

the enlarging optic will increase the degree of magnification at a given column height without changing exposure time. As an example, if a standard 50mm enlarger lens produces an image length of 19½ inches, the image projected on the easel will increase in length from 19½ to 23½ inches if a +3 lens is fitted to the 50mm lens. Switch the +3 to a +5 and you can add another four inches to the overall image length. The same diopter combinations used with a 75mm lens for 6x6cm negatives will increase the image length from 21 inches to 25½ and 28 inches, respectively.

Practical Hints

We're not going to delve too deeply into the use of close-up lenses here—that's a topic for an entire book. However, there are some tips I'd like to pass along at this point to help you get started in using diopter lenses correctly. The more you work with these, the more fascinating you'll find them to be, and the more ingenious your approach will become.

For head-and-shoulder portraits, stay with a +1 diopter lens. If you own a simple camera which uses snap-on filters, you'll probably find that the manufacturer offers a special "portrait attachment" or "portrait lens" to fit it. This is nothing more than a +1 close-up lens encased in a plastic holder which fits over the camera lens.

Use a tripod whenever possible, even with portraits. As I've pointed out earlier, depth of field is precious when working at or in front of the camera's normal close-focusing distance, and you can't afford to waste it by unnecessary camera movement toward or away from your subject at the moment you trip the shutter.

You'll find a copy stand a useful accessory in many situations, such as copying documents, stamps, coins, etc., or wherever a tripod proves awkward to use. This can be equipped with lights to give you a self-contained yet portable camera support.

Use care in positioning your subject when working with a non-SLR camera. The viewfinder sees a slightly different field of view than does the lens, and it's possible to cut off the top or side of your subject without knowing it. Some manufacturers offer special close-up kits which include an adjustable field frame. This is attached to your camera and protrudes in front of the lens to assist you in centering the subject properly.

When photographing small objects such as flowers, use a center spot filter to diffuse extra-neous material in the field of view and spotlight the subject. If the background is really cluttered, try positioning a piece of colored poster board behind the subject. Choose a color that will not clash with that of the subject. You can also shoot from a low angle and use the sky as your background.

With living creatures such as insects for your subject, work with a telephoto lens. The greater lens-to-subject distance lets you position your lighting properly. If working outdoors, you may want to use a white sheet of poster board or some aluminum foil to reflect additional light into the shadows. Use a fairly powerful diopter lens and pick a shutter speed/lens opening combination that will accommodate both depth of field and subject movement with the least amount of compromise.

Try combining diopter lenses with other filters. The less-complex images of 3P and 3R prism attachments will provide interesting effects in close-up work. Light balancing filters can be useful to eliminate bluish shadows outdoors or otherwise "warm" up your subject, especially when using electronic flash or working with light colors which pick up a cast from surrounding hues.

Don't overlook the use of contrast filters with black-and-white film to provide tonal separation between your subject and its surroundings. This can be especially valuable in establishing a visual feeling of depth. Contrast filters are also useful when copying damaged or faded photographs. Table 2 provides a quick summary of copy problems and filters that can be used in solving them.

TABLE 2

FILM/FILTER RECOMMENDATIONS FOR COPY WORK

Original and Condition	Kodak Film	Filter
Faded print with overall yellow coloration; faded documents	Contrast Process Ortho	Blue (No. 47)
Blueprints	Contrast Process Pan	Red (No. 25)
Handwriting (blue ink); documents on yellowed paper	Contrast Process Ortho	Yellow (No. 9)
Photographs with colored stains	Ektapan	Same color as stain

Filter Systems

When you stop to think about it, the system concept of filtration has been around for many years now in the form of filter gels. Yet amateur photographers paid little attention to the concept until the advent of the Cromofilter system in 1976. This was quickly followed by a new breed of inexpensive matte box/lens shades which can be easily adapted to virtually any camera. The success of these applications led directly to the new filter systems now appearing on the market.

What's a System?

Essentially, a filter system is nothing more than an efficient method of using a large variety of contrast, correction and special-effect filters. System design means that all filters provided for the holder are uniform in size and can be used alone or in combination to achieve an infinite number of possibilities. Within the limits imposed by their method of attachment, today's popular screw-in filters can also be considered as a filter "system," but these very limitations reduce the range of effects which are possible.

Attach three or four screw-in filters to the front of your lens and you not only have a very unwieldy mess protruding from your camera, but you also invite vignetting, flare and other problems. A true filter system, however, permits the use of several filters without introducing such problems, since the filters are either gels or sheets of thin optical resin material. These are used in a filter holder which attaches to the front of your lens via a screw-in adapter ring. If you own several cameras which require different filter sizes, you simply buy a different adapter ring for each lens. This eliminates the need for stepping rings or other means of adapting glass filters to varying lens mount sizes.

Filter systems also invite the photographer to create materials not offered in filter form by the manufacturer, permitting an unlimited outlet for his/her creative talents. To this end, let's begin our exploration of the systems approach to filtration with a recap of the filter gel and its role.

Gelatin Filters

Manufactured of liquid gelatin appropriately colored by organic dyes to achieve a specified transmission/absorption quality, filter gels are only 0.1mm ± 0.01mm thick. Since they are so thin, gels possess excellent optical qualities, have little adverse effect on image definition, and offer only a slight increase in the length of the optical path through which image-forming light rays must pass.

Jean Coquin used double masks with the Cokin System to produce this startling effect. (Courtesy Minolta Corporation)

Another Coquin photograph made with the Cokin System and linear shutter. (Courtesy Minolta Corporation)

Although protected by a thin lacquer coating, filter gels are quite fragile and require care in handling and use. They must be handled only by their edges and stored in their original packaging when not in use. If the original package is not available, place them in sheets of clean tissue paper and store between the pages of a book to keep them flat. Excessive stress deforms gels, and moisture will cloud them.

When cleaning a gel, use only a clean, dry lens brush or a few light sprays from an aerosol can of Dust Air or other canned freon gas. Touching or rubbing the gel surface is not recommended. Even with the utmost care in use and storage, they tend to scratch easily and you should plan on replacing them periodically.

Filter gel holders are available to accept the three most common gel sizes—2-, 3- and 4-inch squares. Of the three, the 3-inch (or 76mm) square is the one most generally used. Gels can be bought in this size, or you can cut them from larger-size sheets. Cutting your own is more economical in the long run, and gel sheets are offered in sizes up to 14-inch squares. These are designed for use in front of studio lamps instead of the lens. If you decide to cut your own from a larger sheet, don't try to cut the gel by itself. Sandwich it between two clean sheets of reasonably stiff paper and then use a pair of sharp scissors or an X-acto knife to make the cut to the desired size.

Temperature, humidity and age all have an ef-

FILTERS—HOW MANY ARE TOO MANY?

There are times when it's desirable or even necessary to use more than one filter or special-effect attachment at a time. Disregarding the potential image degradation which arises from positioning one or more optical planes in front of your highly corrected lens, how can you tell when "enough is enough"?

Simply by looking through the viewfinder, is the usual response from most amateurs. Unfortunately, this is not correct—not even for SLR users. The answer varies from lens to lens and depends upon the focal length, the size of the front element, the distance between the front element and the end of the lens barrel, and the f-stop selected for use. The only sure-fire way to determine how many lens attachments you can use at one time with a given lens is to use your camera's depth-of-field preview lever.

After determining which combination of attachments you wish to use, set the lens's aperture at the desired opening. Thread the first attachment to your lens barrel and look through the viewfinder as you depress the depth-of-field preview lever. If you notice no dimming at the corners, thread the next attachment into the previous one and recheck the viewfinder at the shooting aperture. When you do see the corners dim as you apply the depth-of-field preview lever, vignetting is occurring and you've got one too many attachments in place.

But suppose you're using an SLR without a depth-of-field preview lever, or a rangefinder/compact 35mm camera? There's no guaranteed way of determining how many attachments can be safely used in advance of taking the picture with such cameras. Not only are you restricted in terms of the viewfinder and/or lack of a preview lever, but most such cameras have a programed exposure control that makes it next to impossible to determine which aperture the camera will select to take the picture. Your best bet with one of these cameras is to take several pictures using the combination of attachments and keep your fingers crossed. Beyond this, you will do well to restrict yourself to using two filters or one filter and one lens attachment in combination if you want to be certain of getting the picture without possible vignetting.

fect on the stability of the dyes used in filter gels, with some dyes more subject to fading than others. Keeping gels away from high temperatures and storing them in dark, dry places will increase their useful life, but it's still a good idea to inspect them at periodic intervals. Either hold the gel up to a light or place it on a light table and examine the surface carefully from center to edge for uniformity. Since the center of the gel receives more exposure to light than the edges (which are protected by the filter holder), it's the area where fading is most likely to occur. By the time such fading is noticeable to your eye, the gel has long since served its purpose and should be discarded in favor of a new one. Gel fading is more rapid (and noticeable) when the sheet is mounted directly in front of a studio light.

Matte Box/Lens Shade

These collapsible lens attachments are really nothing more than a sophisticated filter gel holder. The adjustable bellows which forms the lens shade is fitted with a slotted holder at the front and a thinner slot at the rear. The front slot accepts a variety of rectangular opaque or translucent masks to frame your subject in odd-shaped configurations—a diamond, heart, keyhole, etc. The rear slot is designed to hold standard three-inch filter gels. Either slot may be used alone, or both may be used at the same time.

Three such units are currently available: the Ambico Shade +, Spiratone UltiMatte©, and Novoflex Proson. The Shade + and UltiMatte, which appear to be the same unit, use 3½ x 4½-inch masks and three-inch filter gels. The Pro-

son is designed to accept Gepe 6x6cm slide mounts containing cut-out masks or colored gels at front and rear. Each manufacturer offers a variety of masks and gels for use with his unit, but you can also make your own. Thin posterboard works well for making opaque masks, while clear acetate can be used for translucent ones.

Masks are offered in both male and female versions for use in double-exposing effects. Consider the keyhole, for example. The female mask is opaque with a keyhole cut out in the center; the male mask is translucent with an opaque keyhole in the center. When these are used together, you must remember to use the same lens opening for each exposure, as the size of the mask and its edge definition on the film changes in size according to the f-stop used.

You'll encounter two minor problems when

The Cokin System with lens shade.

The Kenko Technical Filter Gel Holder mounts to the lens with a threaded adapter ring and opens to accept 3-inch-square gels.

The Acme Multifilt System with lens shade.

using one of these attachments. Since the bellows folds up for ease in storage and carrying, it must be extended for use after mounting to the lens—how much will depend upon the focal length of the lens with which it is used. Each of the shades available has focal length calibrations stamped on the shade rail to help in positioning it properly, but it's also a good idea to double-check your setting.

To do this, stop the lens down to the smallest aperture you intend to use and set the focus to infinity. Look through the viewfinder and check for any signs of darkening in the corners of the frame. If such vignetting is present, readjust the shade length while looking into the finder. Be sure the lens is focused at infinity—its angle of acceptance is smaller at closer distances, and vignetting which may not show at seven feet can appear when you focus on more distant subjects.

The Ambico System with lens shade. Shades are provided in both 35mm and 6x6cm sizes.

The Cokin System accepts rectangular and circular filters in the holder grooves.

The second problem is that of exposure. Since the use of an opaque mask will prevent a high percentage of light from reaching the metering cells within the camera, bracketing is the only real solution. Try a three-picture sequence, shooting a full stop above and below the camera meter's recommended exposure, when using opaque masks. Working with translucent masks is a different matter, as you're actually making a multiple exposure. Because each exposure is more or less independent of the others, you really shouldn't have to worry about exposure compensation under normal circumstances.

System Filters

The enormous success of the original Cromofilter concept (see Chapter 17) led directly to the development of the Cokin® system, first introduced in 1978. The Cokin system has just become available in the United States through Minolta Corporation and already has competition from the recently introduced filter systems by Ambico and Acme Multifilt. These new approaches to comprehensive creative filtration are basically improved, updated and expanded versions of the older filter gel/holder system discussed at the beginning of this chapter.

All use a filter frame or holder of plastic which is attached to the camera lens by a screw-in adapter ring. As used by Cokin and Ambico, this assembly contains two tracks or spring-tight grooves which hold the filters in position. The Acme Multifilt holder contains three grooves. In addition to the use of multiple filters, the holders are designed to permit three independent movements.

Square filters can be offset from the center, while the circular ones (such as the star burst or polarizing) can be rotated *within* the holder. The filter holder itself rotates on the adapter to provide the third type of movement. By combining two or more such movements, you can orient or offset multiple images or control the shading of a graduated filter in such a way as to suit your subject precisely. This feature will be especially appreciated by those who have used the screw-in type of graduated filter, where control is possible only through focal length choice or manipulation of camera-to-subject distance.

The heart of these new filter systems rests in the number and type of filters which are offered for use with the holder. For example, the Cokin system provides some 78 different filters and effects. The full range of graduated and fog filters offered in the screw-in Cromofilter type form the basis of the new system, along with a complete light-balancing set (81-82 series) for color work, and a full contrast set for use in black-and-white photography.

In addition, dozens of special-effect filters are offered—star burst, diffraction, prism, pastels, multiple image, center spot, diffusers, etc.—as well as the various masks and overlay effects previously discussed in the matte box/lens shade concept. And for those who wish to exercise their own ingenuity, there's even a kit containing 20 colored gels and a special filter holder to let you make your own effects.

The uniqueness of the system approach to filtration is best illustrated with a couple of examples. The type of prism attachments which are offered in screw-in mounts will position the images in a given area on the film. Your only means of control, however, is to revolve the prism. This will change the image positions, but only on the same axis. But by combining the filter holder/filter movements possible with one of these three systems, you retain far more control over image placement on the film. For example, it's possible to place the multiple images only on one side of the frame, at the top, or at the bottom—leaving the rest of the area unaffected.

A second example involves the use of the so-called Color Back filters by Cokin. These allow you to modify the color of the background without affecting the foreground by using fill flash outdoors. Here's how it works: Place a yellow filter over the lens—this will give an overall yellow tint to the image. Now fit a mauve filter over your flashtube. Since mauve is complementary to yellow, it will cancel out the effect of the yellow filter on the foreground, but that area (background) not lit by the flash will remain yellow.

The Acme Multifilt system differs from the Cokin and Ambico systems in several interesting ways. The Multifilt adapter ring (called a Skydapter) is available for cameras accepting a 40.5mm to 77mm screw-in filter. It contains a built-in skylight (1A) filter and can be left on your camera lens permanently, providing the same protection as the circular screw-in skylight filter. Metal threads in the front of the ring accept regular screw-in filters which you might own. Since the holder snaps *onto* the adapter, you can use a combination of regular screw-in filters and the Multifilt system.

The Skydapter can also be obtained without the built-in filter, as some serious amateur and professional photographers may not want to use a skylight filter for every shot. Unlike the rectangular Cokin filters, the Acme system uses filter squares. Like the Cokin filters, these are manufactured of CR39© but Acme claims the use of a special polymerization process to impart the transmission qualities necessary. This permits introduction of the desired colors into the CR39 material while it is in a liquid mass state. According to Acme, the polymerized CR39 has a $\pm$ 3 percent tolerance from Wratten standards—ten times that of many glass filters. Because they are dyed-in-the-mass, Multifilt

Below left:
Cokin filters are identified by type and effect.

Below center:
The Cokin filter holder accepts a variety of snap-in threaded adapter rings.

Below right:
One of the more unusual Cokin filters, this multi-image can be positioned to obtain a variety of effects not possible with the standard screw-in prism attachments.

filters are resistant to fading, chipping or peeling of the color.

The Cokin, Acme Multifilt and Ambico systems can be obtained from virtually any photo dealer in the United States. Regardless of the system you buy, my advice is essentially the same as with the chromatic filters—don't start off with the entire system. There are far too many things you can do with system filtration, and experimentation (that word again) is the key to effective utilization.

Having the entire system at your disposal is both costly and confusing—you're better off starting with the holder and a handful of selected filters. Work your way slowly into the system approach by exploring its potential filter by filter—your photography will benefit far more from a step-by-step progression.

Flash Filter Systems

A few years back, flash manufacturers began to apply a system concept to the lowly electronic flash or EF unit. Flash filter kits are now among the wide variety of accessories currently offered for use with many modern EF units. These generally consist of a plastic slip-on adapter which fits over the flash head and is slotted to accept one of the numerous acrylic filters provided in the kit. Depending upon the manufacturer, you'll find several different colors offered, as well as light conversion, neutral density and ultraviolet filters.

Flash filter kits are designed for use with multiple flash setups where creative lighting effects are desired. As such, their use requires a sound background in working with multiple lighting techniques. Used properly, such filter systems allow you to approximate studio lighting effects on a limited budget at home. At the present time, you're limited to the filters provided by the manufacturer of the flash unit; no accessory manufacturers have stepped into the fold at this writing to provide a wider variety of filter types. Those who are serious about the flexibility provided in lighting by flash filter kits may find the type and availability of filters to be a determining factor in their selection of a new flash system.

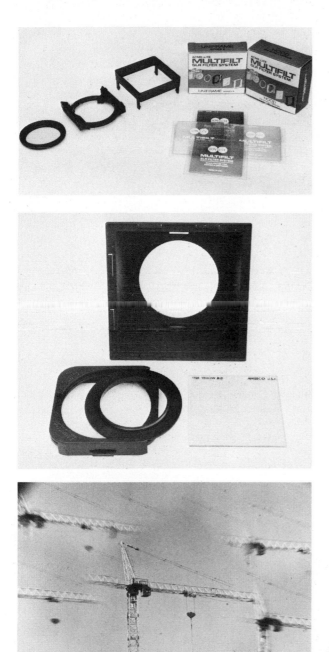

Top left:
The Acme Multifilt system includes the Skydapter, Uniframe, snap-on lens shade and an assortment of square filters.

Center:
The Ambico holder, adapter, shade and K-2 filter. This system also uses circular filters, but they must be fitted to holder before adapter ring is installed.

Bottom left:
Here's what happens when you combine multiple filters with the wrong f-stop. This shot was taken with an 80mm lens on a Mamiya 645. A 3T prism attachment and red filter caused vignetting when the lens was stopped down to f/22. Be sure to check shooting aperture when using multiple filters.

Darkroom Filters

Although they are generally associated primarily with cameras, filters also play an important role in your darkroom. Since photographic film and paper are sensitive to varying portions of the spectrum, you cannot work under normal illumination in the darkroom. If you wish to see what you're doing while processing and printing, the darkroom lighting must be properly filtered. The spectral sensitivity and speed of your film or paper will determine both the color and intensity of your safelight.

Many black-and-white printing papers have a multi-coated emulsion which allows you to control print contrast by means of filtration. All color printing papers require some filtration to achieve the desired color balance in the final print. Such essential filters and their use cannot be excluded from our discussion.

Safelight Filters

Ordinary black-and-white photographic papers are sensitive to blue light only, while variable-contrast papers react to both blue and green. For this reason, we can work under either a red or amber light in the darkroom and see what we're doing without affecting the paper. Since amber transmits more light from a given bulb intensity, it provides better visibility. For this reason, most photographers prefer the amber-colored safelight over the red one.

General-purpose black-and-white films used today are all panchromatic in nature; that is, they are sensitive in varying degrees to all three primary colors. This rules out the use of an amber or red filter when processing black-and-white film. Medium- and slow-speed panchromatic materials, however, have a slight dip in sensitivity at a given point in the green part of the spectrum. This dip just happens to coincide with one of the highest points of the human eye's sensitivity to green wavelengths. For this reason, you can use a very deep green safelight for short periods of time, provided it is kept at least five feet away from the film. Total darkness is required with high-speed pan emulsions.

Some people's eyes can make adequate use of such dim illumination, but for many, the green safelight is virtually useless. It's generally recommended that black-and-white film be loaded into a daylight developing tank, and processing be carried out by the time/temperature method under normal room illumination. Some special-purpose films like Kodak Kodalith are orthochromatic. Since ortho emulsions are not sensitive to red light, they can be developed by inspection under a red safelight.

Below left:
Safelights vary in size and design. These from Arkay can be table- or wall-mounted, and feature quick, easy filter interchange.

Below center:
Typical of the inexpensive "acorn" type, the Kustom darkroom safelight cup interchanges to accommodate different sensitized materials.

Below right:
The Kodak Model B will use either a 7½- or 15-watt bulb, depending upon your darkroom requirements and the type of sensitized materials in use.

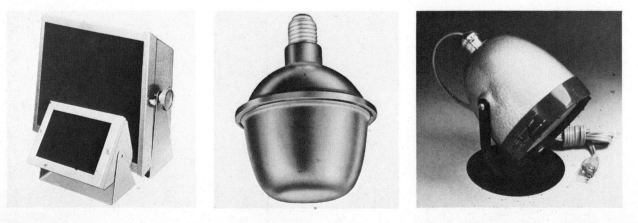

Reversal color films and papers must be handled in total darkness. Negative color printing papers can be used only in a very dim brown light. Unfortunately, this is about as useless to most of us as the deep green light with pan film. Unless you're a professional who spends many hours under such lighting, it's very difficult to tell what's going on under the brown light. Because of this, daylight processing drums and tanks are used for processing color prints and films by time and temperature.

Choosing and Using a Safelight

A safelight is nothing more than a light-tight box which contains an ordinary tungsten lamp and has at least one open side covered by an appropriate filter. Smaller and less expensive safelights often take the form of an acorn-shaped cap of filter material which screws into an opaque base holding the bulb.

Selecting the proper filter according to the sensitized material is not the only consideration in choosing and using a safelight. Intensity of illumination is also important, as is its placement. It's often tempting to replace the manufacturer's recommended bulb with one of higher wattage to provide more light, but this is not a wise practice. Safelights are convection-cooled, and a more powerful bulb will produce a greater amount of heat. This can cause the safelight to warp, which may result in unfiltered light escap-

Below:
Multi-contrast filters are sold in sets and mounted for use under the enlarging lens.

ing. It can also melt the filter, making the safelight a fire hazard.

Unless the manufacturer specifies otherwise, you should keep all sensitized materials at least five feet away from the direct light of your safelight. For general darkroom illumination, one of the larger suspended safelights should prove adequate. Smaller safelights with the appropriate filters can then be spotted around specific darkroom areas. If you want to increase the level of darkroom illumination, point the safelight at a light-colored wall or ceiling. This will reflect the light safely.

How Safe Is Safe?

It's not a bad idea to periodically test your safelight's efficiency to determine if the filter is still suitable for the paper you generally use, if you have located it at an adequate distance from your work, or if the bulb is too powerful. Like all filters, those used in safelights will gradually fade, and while it might have been safe the last time you tested it, that doesn't mean that it will be safe forever.

Occasionally, you'll be told to expose a piece of enlarging paper to the safelight illumination for several minutes with a coin or key placed on it. This will not really give you a satisfactory answer to the efficiency of the filter, since fog caused by a safelight does not always appear on the white border of a print, but just in that area exposed to a white light such as that from your enlarger. Thus, it's possible for your safelight to degrade the quality of highlights in your prints without your realizing it.

To properly test any safelight, briefly expose a piece of enlarging paper without a negative in the enlarger. What you're looking for is a medium gray tone when the paper is developed. Now place the exposed paper in your normal work area or beside the developer tray and quickly cover about one-quarter of it with a piece of cardboard. Expose this to safelight illumination for one minute, then move the cardboard to cover one-half of the paper. Wait another minute and cover three-quarters of it, exposing this final section for two minutes instead of one. You now have a sheet of enlarging paper that contains four test strips, with sections exposed for four, two, one and zero minutes.

Develop and fix the sheet of paper, then inspect it under a strong white light. If the first three-quarters of the paper appears to be essentially the same in tone and the last quarter is slightly darker, your safelight is okay. Any difference in tone between the center two strips and the one that remained covered during the exposure to the safelight indicates that your safelight is too close to your paper, provides too much light, or is fitted with the wrong or a faded filter for the paper you're using.

Determine which of these possibilities may be at fault by the process of elimination. Check the wattage of the safelight bulb—if it's within that recommended by the manufacturer, it's okay. Increase the distance between the safelight and your work area by 50 percent. Repeat the above test. If it still comes out with a difference in tone between the strips, replace the filter and repeat the test again. This should solve the problem.

Multi-Contrast Filters and Paper

Filters are used to control print contrast on black-and-white multi-contrast papers. Such papers have been double-coated, once with a low-contrast emulsion sensitive only to green light, and a second time with a high-contrast emulsion sensitive only to blue light. Exposing the paper through a greenish filter will thus produce a low-contrast print; exposing it through a blue filter produces a high-contrast print. Intermediate contrast grades are possible by exposure through filters which allow both blue and green light rays to pass. The exact degree of contrast in a given print will be determined by the proportion of each color of light allowed to reach the paper.

Multi-contrast filters, however, are not blue and green but yellow and magenta. Green and blue are additive colors. Such filters transmit only a small percentage of the enlarger's light, resulting in a dim image on the easel and lengthy exposures. Since yellow and magenta are subtractive primary colors, they transmit red wavelengths, which make up 65 percent of the enlarger's light. This gives a far brighter image on the easel. The yellow filter also transmits the green wavelengths to which the low-contrast emulsion is sensitive; the magenta filter passes the blue light to the high-contrast emulsion.

Multi-contrast filters are numbered in a sequence. This sequence corresponds approximately to the equivalent paper grades in ordinary single-contrast enlarging paper, but each manufacturer has his own numbering system. For example, Ilford uses 1, 2, 3, 4, 5, 6 and 7, while Kodak uses 1, 1½, 2, 2½, 3, 3½ and 4. Al-

though one manufacturer's filters can be used with another's paper, it's best to use filters and paper from the same manufacturer if you expect to obtain predictable results. When no filter is used, both emulsions are exposed about equally and multi-contrast papers produce a print with normal contrast, just as you'd get with Grade 2 paper.

What are the advantages in using multi-contrast paper and filters? They're especially useful to the occasional darkroom worker since it's not necessary to keep several different boxes of paper on hand to cope with printing flat and contrasty negatives in addition to normal ones. This

A simple filter substitution will change paper contrast when using multi-contrast emulsions.

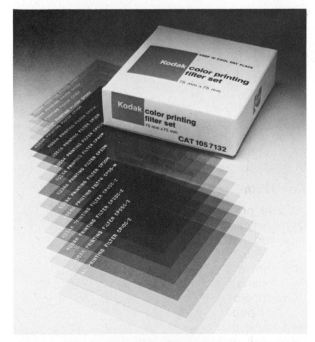

Typical of the acetate type, Kodak's color printing filter set comes in three-inch squares.

(1) reduces your investment in paper, (2) keeps paper storage space requirements to a minimum, (3) prevents seldom-used grades from aging and spoiling, and (4) assures that you won't run out of a particular grade during a printing session.

For the really creative and/or ambitious reader, multi-contrast papers hold still another advantage. By careful dodging, it's possible to print one part of a negative through one filter and the rest of the negative through a different one. Thus, you might soften harsh shadows with the use of a No. 0 filter while dodging the rest of the print, then switch to a No. 2 and dodge the shadow areas while completing the enlargement. Incidentally, multi-contrast paper is most effective toward the low-contrast side of normal; if you need or want prints with a lot of contrast, you should keep a separate supply of No. 5 or No. 6 graded paper on hand.

Multi-contrast filters may be made of either acetate or gelatin. Acetate filters are not optically clear and should be used only between the enlarging lamp and lens. Most enlargers have a filter drawer in the lamphouse to accept such filters. Multi-contrast gelatin filters can be used between the enlarging lens and easel with a special holder which attaches to the lens. This frees both hands for any dodging or burning-in that might be necessary.

Gelatin multi-contrast filters usually are mounted in plastic frames which slip into the holder attached to the enlarging lens. Acetate filters are generally unmounted, as they are used in the enlarger's filter drawer in the lamphouse. Both should be handled with much care to prevent scratching, fingerprints and other smudging. When not in use, the gelatin variety should be stored in their plastic case and the acetate filters returned to their protective envelopes. Clean before using with a negative brush or canned air but do not rub or apply pressure to their surface.

Color Printing Filtration

Color printing paper is used in basically the same way as black-and-white paper, but there is one additional consideration when printing in color. You must control the color of the enlarger's light as well as its duration and intensity. This means that filters are required to obtain the correct color balance from each negative.

Color papers are generally manufactured so that some combination of yellow and magenta filters will usually produce the necessary correction. In rare instances, you might find some cyan filtration to be necessary, but all three are never used at the same time, because the result of combining the three subtractive colors is a neutral density, or black.

Filters used in color printing absorb or reflect a portion of the undesired wavelengths of the visible spectrum. There are three types in general use today—acetate CP, gelatin CC and dichroic—and the manner in which they function and are used differs.

Acetate CP Filters

Acetate filters are the least expensive, most convenient and therefore the most widely used at the present time. They are thin sheets of acetate that contain a certain color dye in a specific, measured density. Unfortunately, acetate has a very poor optical quality. This restricts the use of such filters to a location between the light source and the negative. Most modern enlargers have a filter drawer built into their lamphouse to accept this type of filter. If yours does not, it is still possible to use them by placing the

---

TABLE 1

SAFELIGHT FILTER SELECTION TABLE

Filter Color	Use
Light Amber	Black-and-white printing papers
Amber Dark Amber	Color negative papers; panchromatic black-and-white papers (Kodak Panalure, for example)
Light Red	Slow orthochromatic films
Red	Blue-sensitive films and papers
Dark Red	Fast orthochromatic films
Green	Black-and-white infrared films (except Kodak High Speed Infrared Film)
Dark Green	Panchromatic films (use only for a few seconds after at least half the developing time has elapsed)
Greenish Yellow	Black-and-white contact printing papers; black-and-white reversal materials (after bleaching step)
Dark Yellow	Color print and intermediate films

Note: This table lists general uses for these filters. See manufacturer's instructions for exact recommendations as to safelight color, wattage, distance and allowed time of exposure for a given material.

required filter "pack" on top of the enlarger's condenser.

When positioned inside the enlarger between the light and the negative, CP filters modify color temperature by absorbing a part of the enlarger lamp's output. How much of a modification is made depends upon the number of filters used, their color and density. Dye density values differ according to the manufacturer and system with which they are designed to be used, but are additive in nature. If a filtration change of .60 density in magenta is required, you can add a .40 and a .20 to obtain the necessary .60.

Regardless of the paper and chemistry used, a minimum set of filters for color printing should include the following: one each in cyan, magenta and yellow in densities of .05, .10, .20 and .40. This makes a total of 12 filters thus far. To these, we should add an extra .40 magenta and .80 yellow, as well as an ultraviolet or UV filter for absorbing whatever UV rays might be emitted by the enlarger lamp. This increases your basic filter set to a total of 15 filters.

If you decide to stick with one particular type of color paper and chemistry, buying the filter set offered by its manufacturer will equip you for any contingencies you might encounter, while the basic pack described above might not. It's more expensive initially to buy the entire set of filters, some of which you might never use, but at least you'll have the satisfaction of knowing that you're able to cope with any negative that comes to hand, no matter how challenging.

Gelatin CC Filters

These are used between the enlarger lens and easel in the same way as gelatin multi-contrast filters used in black-and-white printing.

They are generally mounted in a plastic frame and slip into a holder which attaches to the enlarger lens. Because of their location, CC filters must be kept absolutely free of scratches, dust, dirt and other contamination. CC filters must also be kept parallel to each other and the entire pack must be perpendicular to the optical axis of the lens, or distortion may occur. To prevent such loss of definition and flare, it's necesssary to hold the number of CC filters used to achieve the required filtration to an absolute minimum. For this reason, their density range is far more comprehensive than that of acetate CP filters.

When working with CC filters, it will still be necessary to use a UV filter, and some provision for incorporating it between the negative carrier and the enlarging lamp should be made if you do not have a filter drawer. As UV filters are also available in glass, you might try placing it inside the enlarger right on top of the condenser, as suggested for the use of acetate CP filters.

Both CC and CP filters should be inspected occasionally for fading and cleaned regularly to

Many color printing enthusiasts prefer the less-expensive "ring-around," such as this Beseler Color Printing Guide, when determining proper filtration.

The Kodak Color Print Viewing Filter Kit is a handy tool to help "guesstimate" filtration requirements with accuracy.

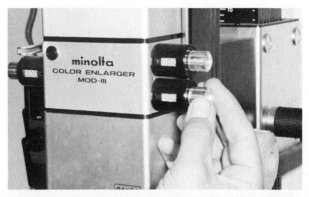

Dichroic filters are controlled externally. This Minolta colorhead contains three-digit counters to indicate how much filtration has been dialed in.

keep them free of all foreign matter. Because of the problem of fading, it's not a good idea to expose such filters to daylight, high temperatures or humidity for extended periods of time.

Dichroic Filters

These are microscopically thin films that have been deposited on a glass substrate by a vapor process and *reflect* the unwanted wavelengths from the visible spectrum. Unlike the acetate CP or gelatin CC filters, which are used in a pack with density changes made by substitution or removal from the pack, only a single dichroic filter is necessary in each subtractive primary color. The degree of filtration with the dichroic type is controlled by positioning of the filter, and so they must be mechanically operated within the enlarger head by a dial on the outside, which is calibrated in fine increments to permit highly precise changes in filtration.

Due to their design, function and operation, dichroic filters are sold as a unit incorporated within a continuously variable enlarger "color head," or a conversion head to replace the one you already have for use in black-and-white work. These special color heads contain a tungsten-halogen lamp and the necessary mechanical linkage, as well as any light-mixing chambers. Light mixing is very important when using dichroic filtration, as the modified part of the spectrum which has been subjected to the dichroic filter(s) must be completely mixed with the unmodified white light that bypassed them.

On rare occasions, you might find that the maximum dichroic filter density provided by the enlarger will not be sufficient for printing a particular negative. If the enlarger head will accommodate acetate CP in addition to its integral dichroic filters (some will, some won't), there's no reason why the two cannot be combined for use. If not, try using a gelatin CC filter below the lens. It may or may not work out to your liking, but it's worth a shot anyway.

Janpol-Color Lens

This European alternative to the use of sepa-

TABLE 2		RECOMMENDED FILTERS FOR COLOR CORRECTIONS	
If print color cast is: [1]		This correction is needed:	To obtain correction: [2]
Yellow	Weak	5Y—10Y	Add 5Y or 10Y
	Average	20Y—30Y	Add 20Y or 30Y
	Strong	40Y	Add 40Y
Magenta	Weak	5M—10M	Add 5M or 10M
	Average	20M—30M	Add 20M or 30M
	Strong	40M	Add 40M
Cyan	Weak	5C—10C	Subtract 5Y + 5M or 10Y + 10M
	Average	20C—30C	Subtract 20Y + 20M or 30Y + 30M [3]
	Strong	40C	Subtract 40Y + 40M
Red	Weak	5R—10R	Add 5Y + 5M or 10Y + 10M
	Average	20R—30R	Add 20Y + 20M or 30Y + 30M
	Strong	40R	Add 40Y + 40M
Green	Weak	5G—10G	Subtract 5M or 10M
	Average	20G—30G	Subtract 20M or 30M [4]
	Strong	40G	Subtract 40M
Blue	Weak	5B—10B	Subtract 5Y or 10Y
	Average	20B—30B	Subtract 20Y or 30Y [5]
	Strong	40B	Subtract 40Y

[1] A weak cast is noticed only in light but neutral areas; an average cast in all but strong color areas; a strong cast is visible over entire print.
[2] Original filter pack should contain only yellow and magenta filters.
[3] Add cyan if required for proper balance.
[4] Add cyan and magenta if required for proper balance.
[5] Add cyan and yellow if required for proper balance.

rate filters for color printing predated the development of dichroic filters in enlarger color heads and has proven popular over the years, partially because of its rather modest price tag for what you get. The lens contains two built-in graduated filters—one ranging from yellow to cyan and the other from yellow to magenta. These are located side-by-side toward the rear portion of the lens.

Knobs on opposite sides of the lens barrel control filter movement and integrate the colors of the filters completely. The knobs are calibrated in CC units up to 120 cyan and 120 magenta, or 240 yellow on each. By using two graduated filters containing yellow, all filter combinations are possible without the possibility of accidentally introducing neutral density.

To many users, the major disadvantage of the Janpol-Color lens is the fact that it must be used at full aperture (f/5.6) for color printing. There is, of course, no restriction on aperture use when enlarging black-and-white negatives. If this concept appeals to you, don't look for the Janpol-Color at your local photo store; many dealers in the hinterlands have never heard of it. Try the larger New York photo shops; they usually carry it in stock in both the 55mm and 80mm focal lengths.

Filtration Hints

How can you tell which color and density of filter to use? This isn't as difficult as it might seem at first, but you've got to get a firm grasp on a couple of facts first. It's only necessary to get one color correct and the others will look right. In most cases, you'll make the necessary color changes by adding or subtracting just magenta and yellow filters, either alone or in combination as required. If filter pack manipulations continually indicate a need for cyan, it's a tip-off that too much infrared radiation is reaching the easel. To solve the problem, use an infrared-absorbing filter (also known as a heat-absorbing glass) under the enlarger lens.

The important point is to learn to identify which colors you must correct and what the corrections should be. Strongly masked negative color films such as the older Kodacolor-X usually required a basic filter pack of about 50M + 20Y. Its replacement, Kodacolor II, needs a stronger red content, and Kodak recommends 80M + 80Y. But the color balance of paper emulsions tends to vary from batch to batch, just as with color film emulsions. For this reason, you may find a note packaged with a new box of paper which recommends an initial color

bias for its use.

If this bias is stated as +30M -20Y and your basic pack is 80M + 80Y, use 110M + 60Y for your initial print. Once you've finished the box of paper and open a new one, reduce your filter pack by removing the bias for the old box; then add the necessary bias for the new box. Thus, if you generally need a 50M + 40Y filter pack and the paper has a bias of -10M + 10Y, your basic pack should be 40M + 30Y.

There are several other things you must remember about color printing filtration if you expect to work with it efficiently and without costly frustrations. The smaller the filter's density number (.05), the less correction it will provide; the greater the number (.40), the greater the correction it gives. A moderate correction is in the neighborhood of .15-.20.

Once you've determined the predominant color in a test print, your correction for that print is to *add* more of the same color filtration to the filter pack. This may sound unusual to those who have never worked with color printing. If the print already has an excess of magenta, for example, why should you add more of the same color? The answer is simple when you give it a little thought—increasing the filtration of the excess color is the way in which you reduce its influence in the final print. Remember, we're working with negative color material. To add more of a given color, subtract a complementary color filter from the pack. This is a more desirable practice than actually adding filters, since it reduces the number of filters in the pack as well as their density, two factors which have a strong bearing on the duration of exposure that is required.

With a little practice, you can get a pretty accurate idea of the exact filtration necessary for a second print by viewing the first one through the actual printing filters. To try this trick, place the filter over the print in such a way that light will not pass through the filter before reaching the print. This should also be at a distance sufficient from your eye so that you can see only the print through the filter.

Now scan the mid-tones through different filter densities until you find the one that provides what you think to be the best correction, then remove half its strength from the filter pack. Why just half of the strength? Because the filter's effect on color printing paper is generally greater than it seems when you view through it. But suppose you're printing on reversal paper; that is, making a print from a color slide. In this case, you would *add* to the filter pack, not remove from it.

Should you find this technique to be helpful, Kodak and other manufacturers offer color print viewing kits which can be used in place of the actual printing filters. The Kodak kit contains six cards and each card contains three filter strengths. When you find the filter through which the print looks satisfactory, directions on the card will assist you in determining which filters to add to or remove from your filter pack.

To put this into concrete terms for you, let's assume that a .10Y filter makes the print appear correct. This indicates that it has too much blue at this point. If you remove .05Y filtration from the pack, you should be right on the mark. One point to remember when determining filtration— you're printing to suit your own tastes. If you find that a slight deviation from normal makes the print more effective to you, don't be afraid to use it.

Remember that filters of the same color combine their densities when added to the pack—a .10M, a .20M and a .30M equal a .60M. But when two different filters are added together, as a .20M and a .20Y, their densities *do not* add up to a .40R, but remain a .20R instead. To keep yourself pointed in the proper direction and avoid any confusion which might otherwise arise, try to keep this fact in mind when correcting color imbalance.

Calculating Exposure for Filter Changes

Filter pack changes affect exposure time. Adding filters to the pack increases the required exposure; removing them will reduce it. If a given exposure produced a satisfactory print density but poor color balance, the same exposure will not produce an equally satisfactory print density once the filter pack has been altered. This is due to two factors—a change in the degree of filtering action and the change (if any) in the number of filters through which the light must pass.

Each filter has an exposure factor, as shown in Table 3. When filters are added, the exposure time should be multiplied by the factor. If more than one filter is added, multiply their individual factors together and then multiply the exposure time by the product. To subtract filters, divide the exposure time by the factor. If more than one filter is removed from the pack, multiply the individual factors together and then divide the exposure time by the product.

If you don't have the factors at your fingertips, here's a convenient rule of thumb you can follow to approximate the effect of any filter or filters on exposure.

A. Add or subtract 10 percent to the exposure for every filter added to or removed from the filter pack.

B. In addition to A, increase or decrease the exposure by a percentage equal to the CP value of each magenta or cyan filter added to or subtracted from the filter pack.

Here's how it works. Suppose you're adding a .20M filter to your pack. Add 10 percent to the exposure to compensate for the extra filter; then add 20 percent more to the exposure because of the .20 value. This means an exposure increase of 30 percent. If you used two 10M filters to obtain the .20M increase, add another 10 percent to cover the use of the second filter, or a total 40 percent exposure increase.

Filter factors are not relevant when working with dichroic filters, as these completely block the wavelengths to which they are complementary, producing virtually no effect upon other wavelengths. Because the dichroic filter modifies the enlarger's light by partial movement into the light beam, as we've seen, there are no additional surfaces to consider when the degree of filtration is changed.

TABLE 3

APPROXIMATE FILTER FACTORS FOR COLOR PRINTING [1]

Yellow		Magenta		Cyan		Red		Green		Blue	
2½Y	1.1	2½M	1.1	2½C	1.1	2½R	1.0	2½G	1.0	2½B	1.0
5Y	1.1	5M	1.1	5C	1.1	5R	1.2	5G	1.1	5B	1.1
10Y	1.1	10M	1.2	10C	1.2	10R	1.3	10G	1.2	10B	1.3
20Y	1.1	20M	1.3	20C	1.3	20R	1.5	20G	1.3	20B	1.6
30Y	1.1	30M	1.4	30C	1.4	30R	1.7	30G	1.4	30B	2.0
40Y	1.2	40M	1.5	40C	1.5	40R	1.9	40G	1.5	40B	2.4
50Y	1.2	50M	1.7	50C	1.7	50R	2.2	50G	1.7	50B	2.9

[1] Make exposure adjustments by changing duration of exposure instead of attempting fractional adjustments of the enlarging lens diaphragm.

Fisheye Converters

Few of the oddball optical attachments designed for special effects are more useful and fascinating than the inexpensive fisheye converter. There are also a number of ultrawide-angle attachments which produce semi-fisheye effects, but these amount to little more than low-cost substitutes for normal wide-angle optics.

When the fisheye first hit the photographic scene some years ago, its impact was tremendous, and scores of accessory lens manufacturers brought out a conversion lens under their own trade names. All offer essentially the same design, appearance, operating characteristics and quality; thus your selection can be based on price with little fear of inferior results.

Fisheye lenses were and still are expensive, but converters can be bought for a relatively low price (hovering around $100-120 at this writing) and enjoyed even if you're on a limited budget. In addition to the price, the outstanding feature of the conversion lens is that you're not locked in to using it only with the camera for which you originally purchased it—adapters can be obtained to allow its use with almost all 35mm and 6x6cm cameras that accept 67mm or smaller filters.

Once you have the proper adapters, the converter can be used with almost any lens whose focal length ranges between 30mm and 200mm, regardless of camera format. For those who already own two or three different lenses for their camera or different cameras and lenses, the fisheye converter can be used with any or all and will produce a different effect with each different focal length.

You'll have to accept a few limitations, but when you compare the converter's price to that of a prime fisheye lens, a couple of slight handicaps aren't really too much to suffer with. Naturally, the first limitation is quality. You can't expect a converter lens to give you the same quality as that of a specially designed prime lens, but unless you expect to enlarge black-and-white negatives beyond the usual 11x14 inches, you probably won't notice any real difference beyond a slight edge softness.

Projecting color slides taken with the converter lens works fine, as long as you don't expect to obtain theater size and quality. And you'd be surprised at the names of well-known professional photographers who use a fisheye conversion lens rather than the more expensive fisheye lens. Since this type of lens has quite limited value to a pro, many prefer to rent the genuine article when they have a need for it and use the converter instead for kicks.

The primary limitation of importance comes in the effective aperture of the conversion lens; this ranges from f/3.5 to f/90 and depends upon the focal length of your prime lens, not its speed. When you attach the converter lens, the prime lens must be opened to maximum aperture and focused on infinity. At the rear of the conversion lens, you'll find a milled ring marked from 30 to 200, and this should be set to correspond with the focal length of the prime lens. To the front of this ring is a cutout slot which contains the f-stop range (according to the focal length setting) and a second milled ring with an index dot for setting the aperture according to the exposure required. So herein lies the real limitation of concern to you—the longer the focal length of the prime lens, the slower the speed of the combination. With a normal 50mm lens, for example, the effective aperture is f/5.6.

As the conversion lens multiplies the focal length of the lens with which it's used by a factor of 0.15X, it turns a 30mm into a 4.5mm wide-

Right:
This is one lens attachment that will provide hours of experimentation and is well worth the slight cost.

Below:
The fisheye converter turns a normal lens into the equivalent of a $1000 optic.

angle, a 50mm becomes a 7.5mm, and the 135mm equals a 20mm equivalent. Considering this and the universality of attachment to most prime lenses, the fisheye converter becomes an ideal investment for the serious amateur who's eager to work in this widest of all areas of photography. You can have a lot of fun without mortgaging anything to pay for it, and if you just happen to trade cameras or buy a second one, it doesn't become a useless hunk of glass—just spend a few extra dollars for another adapter and you're right back in business.

Using a Fisheye Converter Lens

While the advice that follows can be applied equally to the prime fisheye lens, I suspect that

most readers will be more inclined to invest in and work with the conversion lens. More than any other special-effect device, the fisheye leaves the amateur somewhat puzzled as to what to do with it once the newness has worn off. As I've said so often in these pages, the best approach is simply that of experimentation. The more that you work with the conversion lens, the sooner you'll come to discover that certain types of subjects tend to work best with the circular image created on the film. For example, look for objects containing a circular or semi-round design, such as the ceiling of a dome, a winding staircase or even the inside of a pipe. You can also get a global feeling by shooting aerial shots straight down.

One of your first discoveries will concern the

Right:
The fisheye converter attaches to the prime lens by means of a screw-in adapter.

Below:
Setting the converter attachment to the focal length of the prime lens (bottom ring) automatically shows you the effective aperture in the slot.

horizon line. If you keep the lens perfectly level with the horizon line running directly through the middle of the picture, it will remain straight as an arrow, but tilting up or down slightly will cause it to curve; the greater the degree of lens tilt, the more pronounced the curvature of the horizon line.

Attaching the converter lens to your prime lens adds several inches of optics to the package, and although you can hand-hold the body and lens/converter assembly, you'll find it much easier to get good, sharp results by using the camera on a tripod. Bracketing is a good way to determine the proper exposure, but my experience has been that a full stop additional exposure is generally required, especially with color slides. In many cases, you'll have to obtain this by slowing down the shutter one speed (e.g., from 1/125 to 1/60 second).

Below:
Here's the proper way to hold camera, with fisheye converter attached, to prevent camera movement.

Fisheye converters lack the built-in filters provided with most circular fisheye lenses, and there's no way to hang one on the front of the converter without causing vignetting. I've had a reasonable amount of luck using large sheets of diffraction grating or other filter material held in a concave manner so that it can be attached to the rear of the converter with a couple of pieces of cello tape. This isn't the most stable assembly when you finally get it jimmied up, but it does suffice for the purpose—as long as the camera is securely mounted to a tripod.

The key to using a fisheye converter creatively is to let your imagination run wild—place the camera on the ground pointing directly up, photograph a two-dimensional object head-on and make it bend on all sides—experiment, experiment, experiment. However you handle it, the barrel distortion created by the converter will produce striking effects, and once you've learned when and where to apply it, the fisheye converter will become one of your most useful special-effects lens attachments.

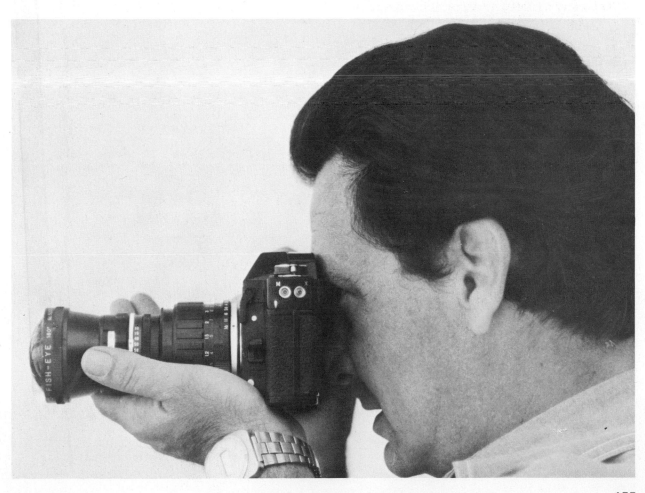

Matte Boxes

The matte box is a very versatile lens attachment which enables you to produce a variety of special effects. A matte box is a combination lens shade/filter holder with a flexible bellows. The flexible bellows allows the filters or special-effects cards to be positioned at various distances from the front of the lens, to provide a variety of effects and freedom from vignetting (having the corners of the picture cut off by the matte box itself).

One handy use for the matte box is as a lens shade that can be adjusted to provide optimum results with many different lens focal lengths. The matte box's flexible bellows can be collapsed for use with wide-angle lenses, to prevent vignetting, and extended with long focal length lenses, to provide maximum protection against stray light striking the front element of the lens and causing flare in the photograph.

Probably the most common matte-box effect is putting one subject in two or more positions in a photograph. This is done by making separate exposures of each portion of the scene in which you wish the subject to appear, using opaque cards in the matte box to block exposure to other portions of the picture. Of course this requires a camera that can make multiple exposures on the same frame of film.

The camera should be mounted on a tripod, because if the camera moves between exposures, the background will not be continuous and the photograph will not appear real. Since each portion of the scene is exposed only once,

Below:
Triple exposure, placing same subject in three places in one picture, was made with matte box as described in text. (Photo by Elissa Rabellino)

and the exposures do not overlap, make each exposure at the same camera settings you'd use to shoot the scene normally.

To make the accompanying triple-exposure shot of the juggler, photographer Elissa Rabellino used a Lindahl Bell-O-Shade matte box and proceeded as follows:

Three opaque cards or masks were used, as shown. The matte box bellows was racked out until it began to vignette the image in the viewfinder; then it was collapsed back about ½ inch to eliminate the vignetting. (This is the best way to check for vignetting when using a matte box as a lens shade, too.) The half-frame and cen-

ter-wedge masks were inserted in the front slot of the matte box, so that only the upper left third of the frame was exposed, and an exposure was made. Then the subject was moved to the right side of the picture and the half-frame mask was reversed, covering up the left side of the picture (which had just been exposed) and uncovering the upper right portion of the scene, where the subject now stood, and a second exposure was made on the same frame. Then the camera was again cocked (without advancing the film—see your camera's instruction book for multiple-exposure procedure), the subject was positioned at bottom center of the scene, and the negative

Left:
Lindahl Bell-O-Shade matte box and three opaque cards were used as described in the accompanying text to make shot of juggler.

Below left:
Spiratone UltiMatte is versatile matte box that permits a variety of effects.

Below:
This card insert can be used with Spiratone matte box to position same subject in four places in one shot. First exposure would be made with card positioned as shown, to put subject in upper left corner of picture (remember, camera is facing you in this shot). Card is then inserted upside down to expose lower left corner. Card is then inserted with opening on other side at top, then at bottom, to make four exposures—one of each quarter of scene.

center-wedge mask was inserted in the matte box in place of the other two masks, thus covering all of the frame except a wedge-shaped section at bottom center. The third exposure was then made. The result of all this, as you can see in the example, is a single photograph with the same subject tossing, catching and ducking the pins.

You can make different-shaped masks out of thin opaque card stock to produce almost any multiple-exposure effect you can dream up by using these basic principles and a matte box. Remember to keep your subject away from the edges of the mask openings, or the effect may appear phony; and shoot with the lens aperture wide open to provide smoothest blending of the edges of the separately exposed images.

Another popular matte-box effect is done with positive/negative montage mask sets. These are pairs of cards, one opaque except for a shape, such as a heart, cut out of its center, and the other clear except for an opaque shape corresponding to the cutout on the first card. By making an exposure of a background (such as a field of flowers) using the second mask, then

Below left:
Translucent cards with holes in center can be used to produce vignetted portraits. Card can be colored with pastels or artists' oils for special effects.

Below right:
Opaque cards with cut-out shapes can be used to shoot picture with subject in shape surrounded by black background.

Bottom:
These cards can be inserted in slot at back of Spiratone matte box (other cards were inserted in front slot) to turn out-of-focus highlights into shapes.

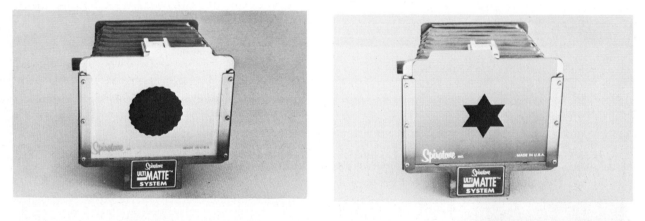

shooting a subject (such as a child) using the first mask, you can put a heart-shaped cameo of the child, for example, into the field of flowers in the photograph. If you want a sharp outline of the mask shape, stop the lens down and extend the bellows; if you want a soft outline, open the lens aperture and compress the bellows. Again, since the exposures do not overlap, use the same camera settings as if you were shooting each scene normally. And again, you need a camera that permits in-register multiple exposures to do this.

Other matte-box effects include vignetting, using either light brown or clear vignetters such as those made for the Spiratone UltiMatte Box. Vignettes produce circular-shaped images that

"float" in the photograph area, eliminating all background detail outside the central image area. These are handy for portraiture when the background is distracting or unattractive. Best results are obtained by using a short telephoto lens (85-135mm on a 35mm camera), shooting at a fairly wide aperture, and using the depth-of-field preview to check the effect before shooting. The clear vignetters can be colored with artists' oils to create colored effects for color photography.

Another matte-box special effect can be produced using Spiratone's Iris Modifiers for the Ultimatte Box. These are 3x3-inch cards that contain such shapes as a star, a heart, a pinwheel, and the like. They fit into the rear slot in the matte box and turn out-of-focus highlights or light sources in front of or behind the main subject into the shape of the Iris Modifier. The effect works best with lenses in the 100-200mm range (for 35mm cameras), used with the aperture wide open.

Matte boxes are versatile lens attachments, and you can have a lot of fun with them. Use your imagination to come up with variations on the techniques just explained, and you'll greatly expand your picture-making potential.

Below right:
Sets consisting of one opaque card with a cutout and one transparent card with an opaque shape matching the cutout on the other card can be used to place subject in the cutout shape in a background of your choice, as described in text.

Below:
Here are some examples of shapes that out-of-focus highlights can be turned into by using cards shown in accompanying photo.

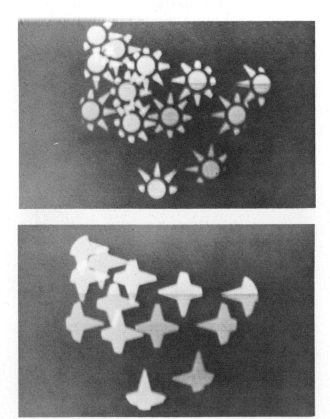

Directory of Manufacturers

The best place to buy filters is your local camera shop. There you can try and compare various filters, and know exactly what you're getting. However, if there is no nearby camera shop, or you are undecided as to the type of filter you might want, write to the companies below and request their current literature, as well as the name and address of the nearest camera store in your area which carries their products. Many of these companies publish quite helpful booklets and brochures promoting their various filters, and they will be pleased to send such material to you upon request. Where a particular filter trade name is used by a company, it precedes the company listing in bold type.

CAMERA FILTERS

(Virtually all camera manufacturers offer a line of filters to fit their various products.)

Asanuma/King
Asanuma Corporation
1639 East Del Amo Blvd.
Carson, CA 90746

Cokin
Minolta Corporation
101 Williams Dr.
Ramsey, NJ 07446

Colorflow
Spiratone, Inc.
130 West 31st St.
New York, NY 10001

Creative Filter System
Ambico, Inc.
101 Horton Ave.
Lynbrook, NY 11563

Cromofilters
Argraph Corporation
111 Asia Pl.
Carlstadt, NJ 07072

Dot/Spectralstar
Dot Line Corporation
11916 Valerio St.
North Hollywood, CA 91605

Edmund Scientific Company
300 Edscorp Bldg.
Barrington, NJ 08007

H & H
Harrison & Harrison
6363 Santa Monica Blvd.
Hollywood, CA 90038

Hoya
Uniphot, Inc.
61-10 34th Ave.
Woodside, NY 11377

Kalimar, Inc.
5 Goddard Ave.
St. Louis Airpark
Chesterfield, MO 63017

Kalt/Kenko
Kalt Corporation
2036 Broadway
Santa Monica, CA 90404

Kodak Wratten
Eastman Kodak Company
343 State St.
Rochester, NY 14650

Multifilt System
Acme-Lite Manufacturing Company
3401 Madison St.
Skokie, IL 60076

Pictrol
Fortune Photo Products
100 Elm Dr.
Levittown, NY 11756

Prinz
Amcam International, Inc.
308 Wainwright Dr.
Northbrook, IL 60062

Rokunar
Aetna Optix, Inc.
44 Alabama Ave.
Island Park, L.I., NY 11558

Samigon
Argraph Corporation
111 Asia Pl.
Carlstadt, NJ 07072

Soligor
Interstate Photo Supply Corporation
168 Glen Cove Rd.
Carle Place, NY 11514

Telesar
Masel Supply Company
128 32nd St.
Brooklyn, NY 11232

Tiffen
Tiffen Manufacturing Corporation
90 Oser Ave.
Hauppauge, NY 11787

Toshiba
Toshiba-Morris Photo Products, Inc.
6435 N. Prosel Ave.
Lincolnwood, IL 60645

Vivitar
Vivitar Corporation
1630 Stewart St.
Santa Monica, CA 90406

DARKROOM FILTERS

Berkey Marketing Companies
Omega Division
25-20 Brooklyn-Queens Expwy. West
Woodside, NY 11377

Beseler Photo Marketing Company
8 Fernwood Rd.
Florham Park, NJ 07932

Colourtronic
9716 Cozycroft Ave.
Chatsworth, CA 91311

Eastman Kodak Company
343 State St.
Rochester, NY 14650

E. I. du Pont de Nemours & Company
Photo Products Department
3300 Pacific Ave. West
Burbank, CA 91505

Ilford, Inc.
West 70 Century Rd.
Paramus, NJ 07652

Unicolor Division
Photo Systems, Inc.
7200 Huron River Dr.
Dexter, MI 48130

FLASH & LIGHTING FILTERS

(Virtually all major flash manufacturers offer a line of filters.)

Berkey Marketing Companies
Colortran Division
25-20 Brooklyn-Queens Expwy. West
Woodside, NY 11377

Mole-Richardson Company
937 N. Sycamore Ave.
Hollywood, CA 90038